Oil
and
Water

ERIC DOUGLAS

© First Edition August 2016 by Eric Douglas. All rights reserved. No part of this book may be reproduced, stored in a retrieval system or transmitted in any form or by any means without the prior written permission of Visibility Press, except by a reviewer who may quote brief passages in a review to be printed in a newspaper, magazine or journal.
All characters appearing in this work are fictitious. Any resemblance to real persons, living or dead, is purely coincidental.

This is a Visibility Press original.
Copyright © 2016 Eric Douglas
All rights reserved.

ISBN-13: 978-1536862812

ISBN-10: 1536862819

DEDICATION

To Beverly: I couldn't get up every morning and write if it weren't for your love and support.

ERIC DOUGLAS

CONTENTS

PROLOGUE 1

CHAPTER ONE 9

CHAPTER TWO 13

CHAPTER THREE 16

CHAPTER FOUR 19

CHAPTER FIVE 23

CHAPTER SIX 29

CHAPTER SEVEN 37

CHAPTER EIGHT 45

CHAPTER NINE 49

CHAPTER TEN 52

CHAPTER ELEVEN 62

CHAPTER TWELVE 71

CHAPTER THIRTEEN 76

CHAPTER FOURTEEN 91

ABOUT THE AUTHOR 96

ACKNOWLEDGMENTS

Many thanks go to my readers who made this story, and make every story, better: Beverly Douglas for helping me tell the story, Danny Boyd for our baseball consultations, Ashley Bringman for your wise additions and Deveron Milne for your detailed and thorough review.

ERIC DOUGLAS

PROLOGUE

To unfamiliar eyes, it was mayhem. Sawdust littered the ground. Animals of every size and description roamed the field. Men and women scurried around half-dressed and in makeup.

But, to a circus performer, this was the real magic of the show. For them, behind the scenes, everything that it took to produce a spectacle under the big top, or in the arenas where most traveling shows found themselves today, was the most exciting part of the show. Acrobats, clowns, gymnasts, and daredevils all came together, from nearly as many nations as existed on the planet to perform. All for that one kid in the front row at his first circus who was just blown away. Seeing his eyes glow never got old for the performers, even when the grind of another city and another hotel bed did. Every performer could tell stories about *that* kid. No matter what was going on around them, the kid would stare, and smile and yell and cheer and cry. That was what made it all worth the effort. That was why they loved it. They never forgot *that* kid.

And that was why they came back to this school each year as well. The choreographers and the designers were elsewhere, in some office somewhere, but when it came time to put together the next year's circus, it was up to the performers to make that vision a reality. Before they could take the show on the road; before they could affect that child in the front row, it took hundreds of hours of sweat, blood, tears and screams of their own.

For Mike Scott, the magic of the circus was behind the scenes as well. He had been one of those kids, captivated by every movement and every trick. He got to be a kid again now that his editor had asked him to visit the circus school and bring home the story of the performers. He was there for the spectacle behind the spectacle. And he was having a blast.

The circus school was at the show's winter home in Florida and Mike was finishing up three weeks of photographing the behind-the-scenes training, orchestration, frustration and work that it took to take one of the world's most famous shows on the road. While circus performers perform and entertain, they are very serious about their craft. Even the clowns spend hours perfecting their antics, pratfalls and jokes to make sure they know them by heart. It takes thousands of hours of sweat and concentration to put together a show as complex as a circus and make it look seamless and easy.

Mike was a photographer for *First Account* magazine. He had traveled the world and photographed great news stories. He had covered war zones, elections and pure terror. But that wasn't what he was about. He was a photographer who enjoyed telling stories with his cameras. The stories didn't have to be monumental or earth shattering. He enjoyed telling stories about people, everyday people who worked hard and changed other people's lives.

He had literally fallen in love with the people and the excitement. These were dedicated professionals of the highest order. Like most closed groups, the performers, animal handlers and stagehands met Mike with some skepticism. They had all seen their fair share of reporters and photographers come to the training ground with an angle or an axe to grind. Mike expected that and used a different approach for this assignment. He didn't even break his cameras out for the first two days. Most of the performers found that odd when he was introduced as a photographer. He wanted them to know that he wasn't there for a quick story. It didn't come easy, though. Several times the performers challenged Mike to see what he was made of.

To see if he was missing something, Mike walked around with one of the circus directors looking at some of the acts that were still in development.

"Leon, what's this thing for," Mike asked. They were passing a 30-foot-tall acrylic tube standing on its end and filled with water. It looked like a display from a large public aquarium where the fish swim in the water column. A set of steep wooden stairs led to a small platform at the top of the tank.

"Oh, that's a new underwater act. The tube is about six feet across inside. Swimmers do an underwater ballet inside. They swim down in twos and threes to the bottom and perform. I know, it sounds a little strange, but it's really very impressive to watch. They stay under an incredible amount of time," Leon said.

"I've done some freediving myself. Thirty feet isn't that hard to get to if you know what you're doing and are in shape, but I imagine that is impressive. On the other hand, I haven't done it in a while and I'm not sure I could do it right now if I had to. Much less spend any time on the bottom doing stunts. Are they going to be practicing that one any time soon? I'd like to watch."

Mike was a scuba diver and instructor as well. After earning a degree in Journalism, he spent a few years living in Grand Cayman working as an underwater photo pro before he decided to return to the world and photograph people. When he wasn't traveling for his job, and even when he was, he did his best to get underwater and go diving. On more than one occasion his job and his passion had intersected when a story had taken him underwater so anything to do with the water intrigued him. A few times a diving vacation had ended up turning into a working holiday as he stumbled across news stories.

"I'm not sure when they're going to practice again. But, I'll be sure to find out for you."

"Thanks, that'd be great. Is that performance going to make it in the show this year? How do you decide what acts are featured each year and which ones never leave Florida?" Mike asked as they walked away from the tank.

"It's interesting you ask that. There is a very involved process where choreographers and designers at our headquarters review possible acts, including the staple performances that everyone expects at the circus – the lion tamers, the clowns, that sort of thing – and decides what else can fit with the theme of the show. Each show has a look and feel and each act has to work with that look. Then they design costumes and figure out how to make it…"

Before Leon could finish his sentence, the men heard a blood curdling scream from just behind them.

"Help, somebody help! Ridian fell into the tank. Someone please help!"

Mike and Leon had walked about 20 feet from the acrylic tube. When they turned, Mike saw a child sinking slowly toward the bottom of the tank. The boy appeared to be unconscious. At least he wasn't struggling or trying to swim. The girl who yelled for help was on the platform at the top. Both children looked to be about 10 or 11 years old.

Mike immediately bolted for the stairs. He knew a circus performer would probably be able to help the boy better than he could, but he didn't know where they were or how long it would take for someone to get there. He wasn't about to stand by and watch the boy drown through the acrylic.

"What happened?" Mike shouted as he ran, taking the steps two at a time.

"We were playing. Ridian said his father was going to let him in the act, but I didn't believe him. We snuck up here as soon as you walked away so he could prove it to me. He was showing off and slipped and hit his head. He just sank." The young girl began to sob.

When Mike reached the platform, he immediately stripped down to his shorts. The sprint to the tank and charging up the stairs had Mike out of breath. He was in good shape, but not perfect condition. He had been traveling too much to exercise regularly. Mike took a moment to slow his breathing and focus on what he was going to have to do. He knew it was going to be difficult to swim to the bottom. Looking around, he saw what he would need to get down. Two weight belts were lying on the platform with five pounds of lead on each one. The performers had been using them to train with.

Mike picked up both belts and draped them over his shoulders, took three quick breaths and did his best to relax and then simply stepped off of the platform and into the water. He knew the extra weight from the belts would help him sink quickly so he opted to descend quietly rather than trying to swim down. He might have made it down a second or two faster by swimming, but he knew he was going to have to save his energy to grab the boy and get them both back to the surface.

The cool water in the tank was a shock to Mike's system. His body immediately began demanding that he breathe, but Mike suppressed the urge and did his best to focus on what he had to do. He knew twisting, turning or struggling would slow his descent and use up the oxygen in his body that much faster. The only movement he allowed himself was to bring his hand to his face to pinch his nose and equalize his ears with the increasing pressure of the water as he made his descent.

Freedivers prepare themselves. They relax. They don masks and specially-made, extra-long, extra-large fins to propel themselves through the water. Mike had none of that. He going to have to grab the boy and swim him to the surface. Without fins or help. He would be cutting it close by the time he got to the surface.

The pressure of the water surrounding him increased the concentration of oxygen in his blood. As Mike ascended, he would be using more of that oxygen. Coupled with the dropping pressure on his body as he swam to the surface, he could potentially black out. He would be in danger of a shallow-water blackout. He might end up grabbing the boy and making it almost all the way back to the surface before losing consciousness and sinking back down with the boy. That would make things even worse. The boy wouldn't make it to the surface to get the air he so desperately needed and then someone would have to rescue Mike as well.

These thoughts flashed through Mike's mind in the moments it took him to descend through the water. He knew he knew it was dangerous, but he also knew he didn't have a choice in the matter. He just hoped other rescuers would be there in time to help.

Landing on the hard acrylic bottom of the tank, Mike immediately began to search for the boy. He hadn't been able to grab a mask before he got in the water so everything around him was a watery blur. To make matters worse, the performers had equipment on the bottom of the tank to use in their show. They would hold on to it or swim around it while performing their underwater ballet. These props broke up Mike's line of sight making it even harder to find the boy.

As Mike searched his lungs began to burn. His mind was screaming that he needed to breathe. Every fiber of his body told him to bolt for the surface. Mike swallowed to suppress the urge and kept searching. He knew he would not be able to swim to the surface and make it back down again in time to save the boy. He had one shot at this and he was running out of time. He was the boy's only hope. And then he saw the small lifeless shape lying on the bottom of the acrylic tank.

The boy was lying against a block that formed the base of one of the performer's supports. Mike dropped to his knees and lifted the boy over his shoulder while he dropped the two weight belts. From his crouched position, and with all of the energy he had left, Mike sprang from the bottom, propelling the two of them toward the surface and air.

Mike kicked with his legs as hard as he could and swam upward with his free arm. His mind was screaming for fresh air. He had no idea how far he was from the surface. Doubt started to creep into his mind. *Can I make it? What if I'm too late? Should I have done this differently? What if I had...?*

Mike's head began to swim and he knew he was close to blacking out.

As his brain started to shut down, his head broke the surface. As he felt the water fall away and air on his face, Mike breathed in as rapidly as he could. A second breath. He was able to focus his eyes. There were people on the stand. Hands reached out and grabbed the boy from Mike. Others helped Mike climb out of the water.

The performers were used to taking care of their own so they immediately began caring for the boy. One rescuer opened his airway and delivered two rescue breaths. When the boy didn't immediately respond and begin breathing on his own, another performer called 911 while a third jumped in to set up an oxygen kit. They immediately began CPR and started giving him oxygen.

After just a minute, the first rescuer rechecked the boy and could tell he had begun breathing on his own. They kept the oxygen in place and watched the boy to make sure he continued to breathe.

By the time emergency medical services had arrived, just a few minutes later, the boy was beginning to regain consciousness. The quick action of the rescuers had saved the boy's life. There was no question in anyone's mind; Mike had saved the boy's life.

Mike would have won the performers' confidence at some point and gotten the story he was really looking for. He was a professional and he took his time and got involved with the people. That was the way he liked to work and he had earned the right. Winning just about every photography award possible — including the Pulitzer Prize for News Photography for a story that nearly ended his career until he found his bearings again – had given him the luxury of doing what he wanted to do when he wanted to do it. Mike would have gotten the story, but his selfless effort to save the boy opened every door and broke down every barrier that anyone could have ever thrown up. They accepted him as family immediately and allowed him inside their homes and allowed him access to their lives without hesitation.

When it was all said and done, Mike uploaded his photos to the magazine headquarters and then relaxed. In the morning, he would climb onto an airplane for a brief vacation before his next assignment, but for one night, he was going to have some fun.

The circus performers were holding a dress rehearsal of their complete show before heading out on the road. Each of the performers had done their acts hundreds, if not thousands, of times before, but this was the final chance for everyone to see how it would look for that kid in the front row with the big eyes. Mike was going to be there for that too, although not as a journalist. For him, the stress and the intensity of the assignment were over. Now, he got to enjoy this last night with his new group of friends. He got to sit in the front row, in the owner's box, and enjoy the show. He got to be the wide-eyed kid again. He couldn't wait.

CHAPTER ONE

There was no place in the world Mike would rather be at the moment than where he was. The assignment at the circus had been great, but he needed to recharge his batteries before his next one. For him, there was no better way to start the morning than staring at the bright blue Caribbean water with the sun rising in his face and a gentle warm breeze coming across the water. The island he was on this time, Curacao, was beautiful, but in some ways it didn't matter. It was all about making a connection to the water. It was a joke, but he felt if he was away from the ocean for too long, his gills would dry out. Mike grew up in land-locked West Virginia, but fell in love with the ocean when he was young. For him, the ocean held promise. It was vast and frightening, but it was also warm and inviting.

From the open air restaurant at the hotel, Mike could see the semi-circular bay with its sugar white sand beaches and to his right, there was a dock where the dive boats tied up. Mike could see the boat crew making the final preparations so he signaled for his breakfast check and took a long last pull from his cup of coffee. Mike stood and stretched. He was stiff from his recent travels. He wasn't 25 years old anymore and it took him longer to recover from long flights. *Heck, even short flights hurt more than they used to*, Mike thought.

"Excuse me, sir. Are you going out on the dive boat this morning?"

"What? Oh, sorry. Yes, I'm going out this morning. Are you guys coming along, too?" Mike was startled by the question, but quickly came out of his reverie to focus on the couple standing across the table. He hadn't seen them approach, lost in his own thoughts. They were in their middle-40s, about Mike's age.

"Yes, we are, but honestly, we're a little nervous," the woman answered. "I'm Myra and this is my husband Doug, by the way."

"What are you nervous about?"

"We've been diving before, but we are still sort of new to it. This is our first time out on a dive boat like this. We go diving in Florida and use our shop's boat, but we've never been diving outside our home group."

"I understand, but don't worry. These guys are great. They'll take good care of you, today. I've been out with them several times and I keep coming back, if that tells you anything." Mike glanced out at the dock and saw the dive boat's captain signal that they were all set. "Looks like they're ready to go. I tell you what. My girlfriend Frankie had other commitments so I'm by myself on this trip. We can buddy up together if you'll let me use you as models for a few of my underwater photos. I promise you I won't be a nuisance."

"I don't know if we're exactly model material," Doug said with a laugh in his voice. It was the first time he spoke.

"Don't worry about that. I just like to have people in my photos."

"Then it sounds fun to me," Myra said. "And thanks." She understood that Mike was taking them under his wing to get them going.

"You're welcome. Come on. Let's go get wet."

#####

"Is the team in position?"

"We are ready and awaiting orders."

"You must stop him before he makes it to the meeting. Do you understand exactly what you need to do?"

"Yes, ma'am. We have men at the point of departure and on the ground at the destination. All contingencies are covered." The man knew his business, but his client obviously didn't. He was a professional, but he knew the people who contracted him and his team weren't always as solid in their determination. They wanted the job done, but wanted to talk about it more than he liked. The man thought of himself as a fire and forget missile. Point him at a target and let him go. He'd get the job done. He knew part of his job was dealing with clients and making sure they were committed to the job, and making sure they paid for the work in advance, but it wasn't something he enjoyed.

"Okay, just walk me through it again, so I know how you're going to do it."

"No, ma'am. We discussed that. It is best for all involved if you don't know exactly what is planned and when it will take place. This is for operational security," the man said. *And better for me and my team if you get cold feet and try to put a stop to things by alerting the authorities. The last thing I need is for you to tip off the cops to keep yourself out of jail,* he thought. He also knew that using terms like "operational security" made his clients feel better about what they were doing. It made them feel like a general sending a team into battle and made ordering a hit on someone seem less like murder. It didn't matter to the team either way, but their clients seemed to appreciate it.

"Okay, okay, I understand."

"All we need now is for your final okay and we will get started. Once you give us the green light, my men will immediately get to work." He didn't add that they would double check the numbered bank account to make sure the deposit was made before they lifted a finger.

"Did you set up the misdirection I asked for?"

"We took care of it."

"Then you have my final okay. Stop Stone from talking to the president. Do whatever you need to do, but it has to happen before that meeting. Do you understand that? It has to be done before he speaks to President Arturo. There is a big meeting coming up and I don't want him to be able to affect that. Do you understand?"

"Thank you, ma'am. My men will get to work immediately. It will go as promised and the meeting in Venezuela will not take place."

CHAPTER TWO

The Gulfstream G650 was the most advanced business aircraft his company owned. It could go farther and faster than any other privately-owned business airplane in existence. It featured the finest in avionics, noise-reducing insulation and had room for eight passengers and four crew members. But Ryan Stone was alone in the cabin. That was okay with him. It gave him time to think without being forced to make small talk. He hated to make small talk. And besides, he really needed to get ready for this meeting. He had all the facts, figures and statistics. That was all done before he left New York. His final preparation had to do with attitude, approach and determination. Stone was headed to Caracas, Venezuela for talks that no one imagined were even possible just a few years ago. He was going to talk to the government of Venezuela about oil production and prices.

Around the world, oil production was at an all-time high. The OPEC nations were producing oil. So were North and South America. The North Sea was still delivering oil, but it was slowing. Overall, consumption was down, though, and those high production numbers were driving the price of oil through the floor. Oil companies were going bankrupt and drilling operations were shutting down. Politicians pointed fingers at each other, analysts pointed their fingers at the Chinese and the American people pointed their fingers at the oil companies.

Of course, the average consumer loved the low oil prices. That meant they were paying less for gas than in years and keeping more money in their pockets. It also meant they could get their gas-guzzling SUVs and Hummers out of the garage and take road trips. They loved those low oil prices until the layoffs started and their retirement accounts took a beating. It was one of the disconnects of the business world that the public hated the oil companies, but loved what their profitability did for the stock market and individual retirement programs that were invariably heavily invested in oil. It was like how everyone hated Congress, but loved their congressman.

Still, there was growing concern about what this overproduction and falling demand was doing to the country's economy, and with it the rest of the world. There was tension in Washington D.C. Their constituents at home were demanding their representatives *DO* something, with enough force and enough volume that the normally reluctant members of Congress were starting to pay attention. They knew free trade was a good thing, and the root of the American economy, but trade in oil didn't seem to be *free* at all. The whole system seemed rigged.

It was a small voice in the wilderness, but there were even those who shouted for the nationalization of the oil industry. They said the price of oil, and its ripple effect throughout the rest of the world economy, was a threat to the economy of the United States. And that made it a national security issue. They called for the US to remove its oil from the open market and keep it all at home.

Stone was the lead negotiator for a conglomerate of oil companies. The various companies, normally competitors, had joined forces to present a united front. His job was to head off the problem before the ground swell of support got too strong. His bosses wanted things to stay the way they were, without too much government oversight. At the same time, the companies were hemorrhaging blood across their ledger books and needed it all to stop.

Venezuela had plenty of oil and it was nationalized. The government subsidized the price of gasoline to provide a benefit to the people. And that was why Stone needed Venezuela's help. Saudi Arabia, as the leader of OPEC, was manipulating world oil markets. They were pumping out all the oil they could to keep the prices low for one simple reason. Hydraulic fracturing, known as "fracking", had opened up the oil market in the United States, giving the Saudis competition. They were flooding the market with cheap oil to drive the American companies into bankruptcy. Everyone expected the Saudis would cut back on production at some point, but no one knew when or how many companies they would put out of business before they did so. The potential economic crisis was the new world order's version of nuclear brinksmanship. Stone's plan was to organize the non-OPEC nations, and get Venezuela to join them, to combat the oil glut. Acting together, they could beat the Saudis at their own game. It might seem like market manipulation, but he believed they were fighting for their very survival.

Stone was shaken from his thoughts by the sound of a *whump* below his feet. The plane was traveling just short of the speed of sound 35,000 feet in the air so he knew they hadn't hit anything. He looked around, confused for a moment, but then started to relax as nothing seemed out of order. Until the next *whump* and then the plane bucked up and down violently.

Stone, like most passengers on private planes, had unbuckled his seat belt immediately after take-off. The plane's sudden moves slammed him into the padded ceiling of the plane's cabin so violently he was knocked to the floor in a daze. The plane was in trouble.

CHAPTER THREE

"Shhhhh, chhhhhh. Shhhhh, chhhhhh."

Mike could hear the "Shhhhh" with each inhale and then the "Chhhhhhh" with each exhale through his scuba regulator. In the space between inhalation and exhalation, he could hear the metallic sound of his exhaled breaths as they tinkled past his ears.

In a week Mike was scheduled to be in Natal, Brazil, off the country's northeast coast, to photograph a group of men, and a few women, who hand-caught lobster using homemade dive equipment. They often ended up with decompression sickness, the bends, and were just as often paralyzed or died. It galled him that his favorite sport was killing desperate men and women who didn't have an alternative. Knowing that job was going to be stressful, Mike decided to stop on the island of Curacao to visit some friends and take a break for a few days before continuing his journey and getting to work. Curacao was the largest of the ABC islands: Aruba, Bonaire and Curacao. Bonaire was internationally known for its diving, but Mike liked Curacao best. The ABC islands were formerly known as the Netherlands Antilles. In 2010, Curacao was granted its independence, although it is still part of the Kingdom of the Netherlands. The nation's capital, Willemstad, was an interesting mix of Dutch architecture and Caribbean color. Just off the coast of Venezuela, the island also boasted its own oil refinery and saw a significant amount of shipping and cargo traffic with goods intended for the rest of the western Caribbean. Shell Oil opened the refinery in 1914 after they discovered oil in Venezuela. Curacao's deep water port was an ideal place to establish a refinery for the crude oil and send it to Venezuela's customers. Ultimately, Shell sold the refinery back to Curacao who leased it to Venezuela.

The reef Mike and new his friends were diving was beautiful. Normally more interested in shipwrecks than reefs, Mike still loved to cruise over the top of a healthy dive site and absorb the sights and colors around him. He was relatively shallow on this dive, only 25 feet below the surface. The water was warm, in the low 80s, so he was only wearing a t-shirt and shorts over his fit 6'2" frame. He didn't need, or want, a wetsuit on this dive. He wanted to feel the water all around him.

Often, when Mike dived in the Caribbean, he liked to put a macro lens on his camera inside the watertight housing. He loved to dive slow and see how close he could get to the tiny, colorful creatures on the reef before they sensed him there and hid in their coral nooks and crannies. This time, however, he had a wide angle lens fitted to his digital camera body that was better suited for photographing the other divers in the water and the bigger reef. He made his living with a camera in his hand, but even on vacation, he didn't feel right diving without his camera.

Mike was following the dive buddy pair he had just met and they had been more than happy to pose for him and allow him to photograph them while they swam. He didn't interfere with them too much, only occasionally giving them directions to swim one way or another. He wasn't trying to accomplish anything on the dive, other than to relax, have some fun and capture some sunshine. They had been diving for about 45 minutes when the couple signaled they were low on air and ready to head to the surface. Mike still had plenty of air left in his tank, but he headed toward the boat as well. There was no reason to push the dive.

Mike's head broke the surface about 10 yards away from the stern of the boat. They were about 500 yards off the northeastern shore of the island, as far away from Willemstad as they could get and still be in Curacao.

Mike waited for the other divers to climb on board the boat, chatting among themselves about what they saw on the dive or discussing how much air they had left. He was quiet, though. He didn't really know anyone on board. So he simply relaxed and floated in the water while he waited his turn to climb on board. Mike turned slow circles in the water while he waited. He was staring at the ocean, away from the island, marveling at the bright blue Caribbean water when he noticed a plane approaching low and fast just above the horizon. He pulled his mask down from his eyes so he could see more clearly. He immediately saw smoke trailing out of the back of the plane. It was in trouble. And worse still, it was heading straight for them.

CHAPTER FOUR

Ryan Stone pulled himself up from the floor of the G650's cabin and looked around, dazed. He shook his head to clear the haze in front of his eyes. He quickly realized two things. First, judging from the way his eyes nearly exploded out of his head when he did, he realized he must have hit his head hard on the padded ceiling of the business jet. The second thing he realized was that the haze wasn't in his head. The cabin was full of smoke.

The G650 bounced around like a dog straining against its master's leash to chase a rabbit down a hill. It would nose down hard and then pull back. It would strain to the right and then flip just as quickly to the left. When Stone opened the cockpit door, he saw the two pilots, a woman in the left seat and a man in the right, focused on their tasks and talking, on the edge of shouting, rapidly to each other and the radio. He could see immediately through the windows in front of them that they were losing altitude and they were still over water.

"What's going on?" Stone shouted as he braced himself in the cockpit door. He had to repeat himself twice to get an answer.

"Sir, please take your seat and strap in," the male copilot answered him, doing his best to sound relaxed and professional. "We're experiencing a bit of a problem here and things are going to be rough for a little while." Stone didn't buy it.

"Guys, there's smoke in the main cabin. I heard the noise. It sounded like an explosion. Where are we?" Stone asked. A trained and experienced negotiator, he was used to seeing past what people said and understanding what they were thinking and feeling. He knew the flight crew might be keeping things under control, but he could see the fear in their movements and hear the tension in their voices.

"Sir, we don't know what happened. All we know is that we've lost control of the right engine and the control surfaces on that side as well. We are losing altitude and need to get this plane under control," the pilot replied this time. "Please take your seat and let us do our job. We are still over the Caribbean, but we are fast approaching Curacao. We're talking to aircraft control and planning to make an emergency landing there."

"But what about..." Stone began but the pilot cut him off.

"Please sir!" Her teeth were clenched as she wrestled the plane. "Return to your seat and strap in tightly. We need to focus on bringing this airplane down safely."

Without another word, Stone moved back to his seat. The plane was descending quickly enough that he felt like he was walking up hill as he clawed his way to the main cabin. He had to move with his hands on the ceiling to brace himself against the jumps and bumps as the plane fought against gravity.

Stone finally got himself strapped in and closed his eyes. For a man who typically controlled his situation from beginning to end he wasn't used to this. He had to rely on others to do their jobs and there was nothing he could do. Stone didn't like his odds, though. For the plane to make a safe emergency landing, they were going to have to level off quite a bit and slow down. The advanced technology packed into the plane didn't seem to be helping at all as the airframe warred against physics. And continued to lose.

Staring ahead at the bulkhead, Stone imagined the flight crew continuing to do their jobs right up until the last minute. Suddenly everything became clear to him. They say your life flashes in front of your eyes at times like this and suddenly everything became clear to him. He was being played.

Years of travel, shuttling from one city to the next hadn't left much time in Stone's life for family or other attachments. Until recently. Heather had come out of nowhere. It felt good to be in a relationship, to have someone interested in him and what he was doing. It was perfect. Until this moment. The clarity in his mind brought on by the adrenaline from the impending plane crash brought something into focus that he hadn't realized before. All of the red flags he had conveniently ignored were there in front of him and he knew what was going on. He needed to let someone know about his epiphany, in case he didn't walk away from this one.

Stone grabbed the phone from the armrest of his seat and began dialing. It took him a moment to remember the actual number since he rarely dialed a phone by the numbers. All of his contacts were programmed into his smart phone. After a couple fits and starts, he put it all together. He hoped the satellite phone system on the plane would connect with everything else that was going on. If there had been some sort of explosion on the plane, it could have fried the electronics and the phone might not even work. Still he had to try. He pushed the button and waited for a moment. Stone almost shouted when he heard it connect and start ringing. He heard the first word "Hi" and then deflated when he heard the rest. "Leave a message and I'll get back to you as soon as I can."

Damn, Stone swore in his head. He quickly recomposed himself to say what he needed to say on a message rather than to a living person. He needed to make sure he said it all and quickly. The message would only last about a minute, and he wasn't sure how long they had left before the plane hit the water.

"I've got to say this quick," he began. The plane began to shake violently. In another part of his head, Stone noted that the drops weren't as sharp as they had been. Maybe the pilot had managed to pull it off and they were going to be all right. He kept talking as quickly as he could. His brain went into overdrive, noticing everything around him. It seemed like life slowed down for him and he was outside of his body, watching himself talk into the phone handset. He could see inside the plane's cockpit for a moment. He saw the two pilots growing more and more frantic as they struggled with the jet. They had done everything by the book, but the plane wasn't responding the way they needed it to. They were going down and both of them knew it. In spite of that, they kept working to level the plane off. If they were able to control the plane well enough they could *land* on the water's surface, sliding along until they bled off their forward speed and the plane settled to a stop.

Stone heard the shout over the plane's intercom as he finished up his phone message. "Brace for impact. We're going down in the water." The plane was nearly level and the shaking subsided for a moment as the pilots prepared for a water landing. Stone leaned forward and wrapped his arms around his knees, curling himself into a ball.

Suddenly everything in the cabin grew quiet and the plane lurched upward. It happened so quickly that Stone was pressed down into his seat. His hyperaware senses knew that unexpected movement wasn't a good thing. Just as quickly as the plane arced upward, it nosedived down and the plane suddenly spun to the left.

It was over in an instant. The G650 hit the water and rolled.

CHAPTER FIVE

"Captain, we've got to move this boat now!" Mike shouted as soon as he got to the top of the swim step and yanked his regulator from his mouth. He was the last diver out of the water and was pointing at the plane hurtling toward them, his dive fins still dangling from his arm. "Look at that!"

The boat's captain froze for a moment when she turned to see where Mike was pointing. Her brain couldn't process what was going on.

"Captain, start the engines, we've got to move! Let's go. I'll get the anchor!" Mike shouted. The authority in Mike's voice jarred Captain Lynn into motion and she twisted the ignition switch on the boat's inboard engine. It roared to life.

Mike quickly unbuckled his scuba unit and dropped it to the deck. He threw his fins and mask on top of it then he pulled a small dive knife from the sheath on his buoyancy compensator. He ran toward the bow to cut the boat's anchor loose. They didn't have time to bring it up.

"We're free, Captain. Move this boat!" Mike yelled as the anchor line broke free with the last sawing motion of his knife.

"Everyone get down and hold on," Captain Lynn yelled over her shoulder. She never took her eyes off of the airplane that was flying toward them no more than 50 feet off the water's surface and 100 yards away. It was coming in fast. She shoved the throttle forward to its stops and the boat's single propeller dug into the water.

Mike grabbed a railing and leaped toward the stern of the boat as the captain got them moving. He wanted to see what happened to the plane so he never looked away. When it was 50 yards away from them, Mike could clearly see smoke pouring from the right side of the airframe; not from the engine nacelle but from the plane itself. The boat had just barely moved from the plane's path when the plane roared past them, close enough that the plane would have hit the upper structure of the dive boat if they were still at their anchor spot. The plane's nose suddenly jerked upward and then the right side of the plane exploded causing the plane to roll to the left. The right engine sheared away from the airframe and the plane crashed toward the sea, its left wing striking the water first and flipping the entire plane onto its top.

Water flew hundreds of feet into the air as the 100-foot-long plane smashed into the water. The right wing broke loose from the airframe immediately on impact. It flipped into the air and landed back onto the underbelly of the plane itself. Within seconds, the shattered shell of the plane was underwater.

Mike and the rest of the passengers stood stunned on the boat. Captain Lynn had pulled the boat's transmission into neutral as soon as they were clear and everyone stared at the scene of the crash. Water, bubbles and debris boiled up from the bottom. Their dive site had been shallow, between 25 and 30 feet from the water's surface following along the top of the reef. From the bottom of the wheels to the top of the tail, the plane itself was only 25 feet tall, but the crash had broken the plane's tail loose. The fuselage was about 15 feet underwater. The normally clear water was completely churned up, though. The divers couldn't see anything from the surface.

"Captain, get on the radio and report this," Mike said, turning to face the younger woman. As a dive boat captain on a resort island, the biggest emergency she was used to dealing with was a bleeding passenger. "Come on, Lynn," Mike said, talking to the captain in a softer voice. "This is an emergency. We've got to call this in. And then get us over there. There might be survivors in the water."

"Thanks, Mike," Captain Lynn said, breaking free from the daze that gripped her. The captain grabbed the radio and started calling the accident in to the local coast guard authorities. They obviously knew about the plane in trouble. The pilot and copilot had been talking to the air traffic controllers at Willemstad's airport. Lynn was able to give them the exact coordinates of the wreck, though. While Lynn spoke on the radio, Anton, the boat's divemaster took the helm and eased the boat toward the crash site while the passengers looked over the side for any signs of life.

"Let's get our gear on and get in there. We can save someone!" one younger man said.

"You're not going anywhere," Mike replied, looking the man in the eyes. "It's not safe. There is leaking fuel all over the water. Even if you could get inside the plane, we don't have lights and any other equipment to see what's going on. You would get trapped and die inside."

"But what about," the man started to argue, but Captain Lynn found her strength and cut him off. "Mike's right. You're all my responsibility and no one is getting off this boat. The coast guard is on the way. They'll be here in just a few minutes. They ordered me to keep you all on the boat and that's what I'm doing," Lynn said. "The island coast guard has a dive team and they're on the way, too."

"Someone could still be alive in there," a woman said, quietly. "Couldn't they?" She looked at Mike.

"Honestly, I doubt it. You saw how hard the plane hit and then it went straight to the bottom. Anyone still inside of that plane probably died on impact from the forces on their body," Mike explained.

"That's why we need to get in there now!" the first man argued.

"First rule of rescue. You have to make sure the scene is safe for you to enter. If you don't, you'll just add someone else that the professional rescuers have to take care of," Mike explained. "Even if we could get in the water this second, it might still take us 10 minutes to get inside the plane."

"I think I see something!" a woman passenger yelled while pointing at something floating 20 feet away from the dive boat. "Is that a person?"

Captain Lynn slowly turned the boat in the direction where the woman was pointing. They quickly realized she was right; it was a person. Judging by the length of the blonde hair floating out around the head and the smaller body frame, they realized it was probably a woman. Mike and the divemaster moved toward the stern of the boat as Lynn cut the engines. Anton jumped into the water before Mike could stop him. He grabbed the woman and swam her over to the swim step on the stern of the boat. Working together, Mike and Anton rolled the woman over, face up, and dragged her into the boat.

"Lynn, get me the first aid kit," Mike ordered as he moved the unconscious woman onto the deck. She was cut and bleeding from several places on her face and head and on her shoulders as well, but none of those injuries appeared life threatening. Mike looked her over for a second. She wasn't breathing. He grabbed a pocket mask from the first aid kit and moved to the woman's side and began giving chest compressions. No one on deck moved while they watched him work. Everyone was still and quiet, willing the woman to live.

Mike completed his 30th chest compression and leaned over with the mask to deliver two breaths. The first one went in. As he started to give the second breath, the woman began to cough and then she took a breath so deep that her back arched off the boat deck. Her body slowly relaxed and sank back down. She began breathing normally, but didn't regain consciousness.

"Lynn, where's the coast guard?" Mike said a moment later, his voice quiet.

"They're on the way, should be here any second."

"Any other survivors?"

"No one's spotted anything," Lynn said, shaking her head, although admittedly most of the passengers had been watching Mike perform CPR on the woman they fished from the ocean. She was wearing a uniform that indicated she was part of the flight crew, and sported a name tag that simply read "Anderson".

A large rigid inflatable boat came buzzing around the corner of the island, nearly flying across the water's surface. It was the citizen rescue group's fast approach boat. While the tiny island nation was patrolled by boats from the Dutch Navy, and have its own coast guard as well, the citizen's rescue organization called CITRO was a largely self-financed group of volunteers who responded to in-water accidents around the island. They carried first aid and rescue equipment on board, along with dive gear to perform in-water searches.

The CITRO members had conducted searches and recovered bodies all around the island. They had even dived on more than one plane that crashed near the island, but never one of this size and caliber. The instructions the volunteers received from the Curacao government as they were dispatched told them to perform a quick search for survivors and then to secure the scene for investigators. From the emergency calls to the air traffic control tower at Curacao International Airport, everyone involved knew the plane was from the United States and carrying an important passenger. They also knew that a crash with a US flag aircraft would bring in inspectors from the US National Transportation Safety Board (NTSB) and more than likely a visit from the US Coast Guard.

CHAPTER SIX

It took some doing, and pulling of strings in both the government houses in Willemstad and the United States, aided in large part by his editor in New York, but Mike finally received permission to dive with the island coast guard team as they searched the wreckage and prepared to bring the downed aircraft to the surface. Mike had permission to be in the water for the dive, but they had given him strict rules as well. He wasn't to enter the aircraft until the recovery team gave him permission and he wasn't to touch anything while he was down there. The local authorities considered the crash site a crime scene and they were making sure no one fouled it up. Especially an out-of-town journalist who happened to be diving where the plane went down.

Mike had no intention of messing up the scene, but the instant the plane went down, he switched from tourist diver mode to journalist mode. He was on the clock and wanted to see what had happened. It wasn't the first time he had stumbled across a story, being in the right, or wrong, place at the right time, but he never worried about that. If it hadn't been for the terrible accident and loss of life in the crash, Mike would have been excited about the opportunity to watch the recovery process and to be there when they found out what brought the plane down. Even though he loved being in the islands, Mike often felt a bit lost without a purpose. He needed something to do to keep his mind challenged. And this definitely fit the bill.

The Curacao coast guard had recruited more divers, along with CITRO, and a several local dive boats from the local dive community for the search and recovery operation. The rescue team would penetrate the aircraft and bring out the two bodies still inside. The volunteer divers would search for pieces of the plane that had broken off in the crash and map their location. They all hoped nothing had come loose from the plane earlier than its contact with water. The location where the jet first reported problems was several miles out to sea and in more than 2000 feet of water.

The Curacao government, on the advice of the NTSB, contracted with a group of commercial divers from the oil refinery trained in salvage techniques to lift the plane from the ocean floor. The commercial divers were to use air-filled lift bags to get the plane off the reef. Then they planned to tow it behind one of the bigger boats to a dock where they had heavy lift cranes they could use to get the plane out of the water and onto dry land.

Mike waited until the three teams of divers entered the water before he stood up on the stern of the dive boat in his dive gear and made his way to the swim step. Mike had been diving since just after he graduated from college, so he was comfortable in a lot of different gear configurations. Depending on the situation, he often had to rely on whatever dive equipment was available, but when he planned to be working underwater he brought along an Ocean Management Systems back inflation BCD with removable wings. Since he had planned to head to Honduras after his stopover in Curacao, he had his working gear with him. The BCD is the piece of dive gear that holds everything else together. It serves as a harness that holds the tank in place on the diver's back and then connects the breathing regulator to the tank. One of the primary purposes of the BCD is to help the diver float weightlessly in the water column by adjusting his buoyancy.

At the water's edge, Mike made one last check of his gear before he settled his mask into place and took a breath from his regulator. He thought quickly about the scene below him. There were two dead bodies in the water and they had been there for nearly 24 hours. He knew they weren't going to be pretty. It wasn't the first time he had seen a dead body in the water, but it wasn't something he ever expected to get used to.

Mike was on the same dive boat from the day before. It, and its crew, had been pressed into service to handle logistics and to get the dive teams where they needed to be. Mike gave a final nod to Captain Lynn who was staying on board the boat and would check all of the divers in and out of the water, and then he stepped out into space and splashed back into the warm Caribbean water. He bobbed to the surface for just a minute to reclaim his digital camera in its underwater housing from Lynn before he released the remaining air in his BCD and began sinking toward the bottom.

In the few minutes Mike stayed on the surface after the dive teams jumped in, they had already organized themselves and were setting to their tasks. Mike wanted to see inside the plane, but he knew he was going to have to wait on that, so he let his photographer mind take over and began photographing the scene in front of him. He knew his editor was going to want to see everything that happened. Mike took some wide-angle shots of the damaged plane resting on the reef. He noted there were still air bubbles trailing toward the surface from the broken fuselage. The water had cleared out from when the plane first crashed, but Mike could tell there was fuel and debris floating all around him. It gave the plane an eerie appearance in the gloom, even though it was a bright and sunny morning topside. It reminded him of the many shipwrecks he had photographed over the years, looking both natural and totally out of place at the same time.

Mike moved to the sand and reef bottom so he could photograph the dive team that was searching for debris and evidence that had been ejected from the airplane as it crashed into the water. The impact had ripped the right wing off of the main fuselage, so small parts littered the reef for a few hundred yards to the east of the plane's final resting place. The search would be exacting, pain-staking work and would take multiple teams of divers days to complete. The very nature of the coral reef worked against them, giving the pieces hundreds of places to hide. The divers were going to have to search every inch slowly and carefully. On this first dive, the dive teams were simply laying out a grid pattern underwater and using small marker flags to identify larger pieces. Researchers from the NTSB would use their computer models to reconstruct the plane and then work backward through the crash. Based on the final resting place of each part, they would be able to visualize the forces at work on the plane while it was still in the air and once it hit the water. Mike imagined he would end up making two or three more dives to follow the search teams to get a complete picture of that work. Mike wasn't the only photographer in the water. The coast guard had recruited underwater photographers and videographers from the local dive community to capture everything that happened as well.

As Mike rounded the plane, he was stunned to see the damage to the right wing. Or, rather, where it had been attached. Mike had covered wars and seen the wreckage after bombs went off. He instantly recognized the tell-tale signs of a blast that originated from inside the plane, bending the aluminum skin of the private jet outward. It didn't appear to have been a large blast, but it was enough. The force of the near—Mach speed and the descent toward the airport did the rest of the work. The plane and the people on-board didn't stand a chance. The pilot's survival was a miracle.

Mike moved in close to the site of the explosion and began take close ups. He doubted the magazine could use those images in the story, but he planned to give a copy of everything he took to the investigators as well. Maybe they could find something.

Mike realized something was out of place. In a high tech airplane, the last thing he expected to see was fine calligraphy. There were diagrams and arrows in the twisted metal, along with printed labels identifying specific parts and pieces, but script? That didn't make sense. Mike repositioned the external strobe lights on his camera to get directly inside the opening in the fuselage. He took several photographs and then checked the images in the LCD screen on the back of his camera. Mike didn't know what it said, but he knew what it was. The writing looked like Arabic script. Had he found part of the bomb? Did the bomber leave a message? Mike touched a control on the back of the underwater housing and zoomed in. He was sure of it. It was some written message and it was definitely Arabic.

Out of the corner of his eye, Mike saw movement and jumped backward, his breath caught in his throat momentarily. And then he relaxed in spite of what he saw. It was death coming at him, but at least it wasn't coming for him. One of the divers who had gone inside the downed plane was pushing a body out through the opening in a black plastic body bag. The diver had added some air into the bag to float the body and he was pushing it out ahead of him. Mike moved to the side and let the diver pass by with his burden. There was nothing pleasant about recovering a body from the water, but it had to be done. A moment later, another body bag appeared in the opening escorted by a diver.

Mike caught the recovery diver's eye as he appeared from the plane. Mike gave him a universal signal for divers. *Okay?* He signaled with his thumb and his forefinger in the shape of a circle. The diver replied with the same signal and then gestured at the body bag. He raised two fingers and then waggled them back and forth. Mike interpreted that to mean that there were only two bodies inside the plane. Mike had called his office and their investigation into the crash said there was only a flight crew of two on board with a single passenger. The passenger's name was Ryan Stone. All they had given him were the last names of the flight crew. The pilot was Anderson and the co-pilot was Milne. The pilot had made it to the surface so two bodies was exactly what they had expected. Of course, no one expected the plane to crash either, so it wouldn't be a complete surprise if there was an extra person on board, either.

The coast guard diver jerked his thumb back toward the plane and then began swimming toward the surface with the deceased. Mike nodded his understanding. Once the diver was clear, Mike entered the airplane.

Entering the plane was momentarily disorienting. Mike had dived in caves and inside shipwrecks, even inside an airplane before, but the experience of entering the airplane resting on its roof was hard to process for a few moments. Everything that was supposed to be on the floor was on the ceiling. Seats hung from the roof like odd light fixtures and decorations. Mike had to turn off his expectations and focus on what was in front of him. He made a mental note to tell the magazine photo editor that the plane was upside down though. He didn't want them to publish a photograph upside down.

Mike began taking photos of the interior and did his best to keep one of the remaining rescue divers in the shots, preferably with their exhaled breath flowing upwards, for reference. The only lights inside the cabin were the high-powered underwater lights held by the recovery divers and the daylight entering the cabin through the portholes along with the gaping hole in the side of the plane.

Whoever set the bomb, and Mike was sure it had been set, had positioned it so it would tear through the outer skin and tear off the wing sending the plane to its doom.

With the bodies out of the way, it was time to start looking for obvious signs of what caused the crash. The recovery divers were examining the entire plane for evidence, but they were paying particular attention to the wrecked side of the fuselage. The blast from the bomb hadn't penetrated the cabin. Mike wondered if the bomber had planned on the crash happening so close to the island or if the blast was supposed to happen farther out to sea. One reason for the directional charge might have been to keep the flight crew from reporting an explosion. The way it happened, they would only know that they had a structural failure. A blast that entered the cabin would be reported over the radio as a bomb.

Hovering inside the topsy-turvy airplane, Mike decided to go see the pilot in the hospital and see what she remembered from the crash. He knew there was a better-than-even chance that she might not remember anything, but he thought it would be interesting to ask the question. Of course, he knew he was going to have to stand in line behind the NTSB investigators. And they might not like him asking questions of their one material witness.

Mike backed into the passenger cabin of the Gulfstream. He thought about what went through the passenger's mind in the last moments before the crash. Mike often put himself in that frame of mind when he dived on shipwrecks, wondering what the sailors on board were thinking at the end. Mike looked at the seat where the passenger had been sitting. It was obvious because the recovery divers had used a knife to cut his seat belt lose to remove the body. Mike noticed a built-in phone that was surely connected to the plane's satellite system. It was off its cradle and freely. Did Stone have family? Did he try to reach out to someone? Something else to look into; did Stone make a phone call and to whom? It might have been an "I love you" phone call, but it was still worth checking out.

Looking upward, past the floating phone handset, at what would have been the floor, Mike saw a satchel tucked underneath a seat. It was an open-topped briefcase that appeared well-worn. Mike moved closer and raised his camera to his eye. Some papers were sticking out of the opening in the case. Mike wasn't about to tamper with evidence, but it wouldn't hurt to photograph the case in place. The paper on of the bundle sticking out of the case had a letterhead that Mike vaguely recognized as an oil consortium. Below that, Mike could see the letter was addressed to "Dear Mr. President Arturo," and then there were some basic greetings, but that was all he could see. Mike knew President Arturo was the president of Venezuela. Stone was rubbing elbows with some powerful people. Whether that had anything to do with the plane crash was yet to be determined.

A flashlight beam flashed across Mike's eyes and brought his attention back to the here and now. The police diver signaled to him that it was time to head to the surface. They had done everything they could while the plane was underwater and he had to leave with them.

CHAPTER SEVEN

The team leader checked his secure email and wasn't pleased to see an email from his last client. It was a request for a phone call. This client just didn't understand how these things went. The job hadn't gone exactly as planned, but it was ultimately successful. The passenger on the private airplane didn't make it to his meeting and that was the job. The plane made it closer to land than they planned, but that was the vagaries of air travel. A tail wind, when they planned for head winds, got the plane across the Caribbean sooner than expected. Still, it would be days, or weeks, before the investigation was over. And by then, it would be too late for the authorities to do anything.

As far as he was concerned, the job was done and there were no refunds in this business. If the plane had made it to Venezuela, that would be a different story, but since it didn't, the job was over.

With a sigh, the man dialed his scrambled phone to contact the client. Regardless of the finality of the job, he was still going to have to explain it. He listened to the scrambling technology work its magic.

"It's me."

"Oh, good. I hoped you would get my message. Thank you for calling." The woman sounded excited and worried, but not angry.

"What is it?" The team leader did his best to keep his own comments to a minimum. "The job was successful."

"You are right. You did the job as instructed. But, I need you to do another job for me. Actually, two jobs. The pilot survived and the plane crashed close to Curacao."

"Yes, I saw that. What do you need done?" The team leader wished the client wouldn't give out details like that. *I need to teach a class in how to hire a mercenary*, he thought.

"I need you to delay the authorities' efforts to recover the plane. Just for a few days until after the meeting. And, we feel that there should be no survivors. We need you to take care of the pilot."

"I see. That will be two jobs, you're right. It's likely that the pilot will be guarded."

"Do whatever you need to do. We just want to make sure there are no loose ends."

"Why is the pilot so important to you?"

"Stone made a phone call from the plane just before it crashed. The pilot may know who he called and that information cannot get out. There can be no threads to tie this back to us. Before she goes away, I need you to find out if she knows anything or told anyone."

"We can handle the interrogation, but you know either way, whether she knows anything or not, we have to make her go away. There's no turning back from something like that." The man thought for a moment his client might have second thoughts about killing the innocent pilot.

"That is what I expect of you. I need to know how to handle things if she knew anything, possibly wrote it down or told someone else. If you can, cover it up. Make it seem like an accident or a suicide. If not, do it anyway.

If she is with someone and it seems like they are more involved than simply bringing her coffee, I need to know about that, too."

"Are you prepared for how far this could go?"

"The outcome of your actions will shake the world. It has to happen. A few lives are simply collateral damage."

The man smirked to himself. This client certainly didn't need any hand holding. She was ruthless.

"I will have the team on the ground get to work immediately. I'll have to hire a local to take care of the plane. There are always men who can use a little extra money in their pocket. There's no way we can get there that quickly and get on the dive team that fast. I will send you a secure email with our fees. The fees are non-negotiable."

"I'll pay whatever you need. Just get it done. Today."

#####

Mike swam from the dim interior through the gaping opening in the side of the plane and blinked a few times. The bright sunshine filtered through the shallow water and it took his eyes a minute to adjust. Looking around, Mike was amazed by the amount of work the dive teams outside the plane had already accomplished. The plane was rigged and the lift bags were in place that would allow the dive team to float the plane to the surface. Mike checked his own air supply and was happy to see that he had half a tank of air left. The shallow depth of the reef was working in his favor. He would be able to stay in the water and watch the plane rise off the bottom at least.

Mike saw they had secured two rectangular 22,000-pound lift Subsalve salvage pontoons to the fuselage of the airplane along with several smaller lift bags at key points around the structure. Those lift bags were mainly for stability, both on ascent and on the surface. They didn't want to the plane to tip or roll once it was off the bottom. Once they floated the plane, they planned to come back for the wing that had broken away on impact.

The commercial divers had already inflated the smaller lift bags and were waiting on the all-clear before inflating the larger salvage pontoons that would bring everything to the surface. As soon as Mike moved away from the plane, the safety diver in charge of all the activities underwater gave the lift team the signal. He was the last one out of the way. Many of the divers stayed in the water to watch the plane rise. Mike moved off to where the rest of the dive team was positioned to photograph that final step from underwater.

The process was slow. The commercial divers knew their business and took their time inflating the primary salvage pontoons. The last thing they wanted to do was overinflate them and then have the plane lurch from the bottom and rocket to the surface. The physics from the pressure of the water would cause the air inside the lift bags to nearly double in volume from the 25-foot depth where they were filled to the surface. Overfilling them underwater to get the plane moving would cause the expansion on ascent to get things out of control quickly. It could put the recovery divers, and the potential evidence in the plane, at serious risk.

Waiting for the plane to move was frustrating for the divers in the water. They wanted to see *something* and watching the commercial divers slowly add air into the lift bags made them impatient. To stay off of the reef, damaged though it was from the plane crash, most of the divers were hovering in the water column. As the anticipation grew, some of them began to drift forward. A few wanted to get a closer look at what was going on while a few others moved in without thinking about it. They simply weren't paying attention to their position.

All eyes were on the broken fuselage when it finally broke free from the reef and began its slow rise. There was a great muffled cheer from the divers watching the scene as they shouted through their regulators. A few of the divers who had been recruited by the police and the coast guard to photograph the recovery process moved in closer. They wanted to capture the plane's first movement. Mike watched the scene and took some of the same photos as the other photographers, but he stayed back a little farther than they did. He knew the potential danger of getting too close to an object being lifted in the water. *The safety diver really should move these people back*, Mike thought. The problem was there was no underwater communication system. They had rushed to get the job done, so there was no way for them to signal everyone to move out of the way without physically swimming to each diver and giving signals about where they should be for safety. That would be slow and tedious as some would understand and others would refuse. The lift was short. Mike just hoped it would go without incident.

The plane inched toward the surface. Its progress was slow at first, nearly imperceptible, but it began to move faster. The water inside and outside the plane had weight. To lift the plane out of the water, they would have to get the plane to the surface and then float it halfway above water. From there, they would have to pump the remaining water out of the fuselage. If they didn't, the weight of the water inside the aluminum structure would tear the plane apart once the crane began pulling on it.

About halfway to the surface, Mike's gut told him something was out of place. He quickly scanned the scene, but nothing set off any alarm bells. The commercial divers in charge of the lift were moving from lift bag to lift bag checking the connections and the integrity of the bags. One of them breaking and dumping its air at this point in the lift could be devastating. If the load were to shift suddenly, there would be no way to stop the plane from tumbling back to the bottom. Mike continued to look from potential trouble spot to trouble spot. And then he found it.

The strap on the lift bag near the opening where the right wing had been appeared to be tearing. Mike thought it would be almost understandable if a strap broke because it was rubbing against the metal structure of the airplane, but this break was happening near the base of the bag itself. The bag was going to fail and there was nothing he could do about it.

The commercial divers had all moved away from that particular lift bag while they made their rounds to the other ones. Mike started to swim in close to the plane and signal the lead diver that they needed to stop the lift. He thought that if they could let the air out of the lift bags and lower the plane back to the bottom before the strap on the damaged bag broke, they could try again after replacing the bag.

Then Mike saw the other problem. One of the photographers had moved into a position below the plane so he could get a unique image of the lift. If the lift bag broke free, the plane could roll and fall directly on top of him. There was no choice. Mike had to get to the diver first.

Mike was about 20 feet away and in the middle of the water column from where the plane had rested just minutes before so he began kicking for the bottom as quickly as he could. He dropped his camera in a sandy area on the bottom so he could move faster and then pushed forward to get to the man, oblivious to the danger he was in. Just before Mike reached the diver, he heard the sound he was hoping wouldn't come so quickly. The strap breaking sounded like an out-of-tune bow string being plucked by a giant's hand. Then Mike heard the lift bag itself shoot for the surface. It all happened in the blink of an eye, but since he was already expecting it to happen, Mike knew what it was. *What caused the Kevlar belt on the belt to fail so quickly?*

The other divers in the water were too shocked by the sight of the lift bag breaking away to do anything about it even if they could have. As soon as the lift bag blew away, the weight of the plane shifted. The entire lift was in trouble.

Mike got to the diver on the bottom. The man was still unaware of the danger he was in and Mike didn't have time to signal to him that anything was wrong. He simply grabbed the diver by the tank valve behind the man's head and pulled him off the sandy floor like a mother dog lifting an errant puppy. Mike planted his fins on the bottom and the leapt away dragging the photographer with him. Mike got the man 10 feet away from the plane and then the other diver wrestled out of Mike's grip and turned on him. The man tried to take a swing at Mike, but Mike blocked the punch easily. Floating in the water makes it almost impossible to deliver a blow. You're not anchored to anything to leverage yourself forward, so your swing also pushes you backward. Add to that the density of the water around them, as compared to air, and there was no danger of the punch doing any damage even if it had landed. Mike pointed at the diver's eyes with both fingers and then gestured hard at the plane. Then Mike made a slashing gesture across his own throat. The signal usually meant "out of air" but Mike hoped the photographer would recognize it as "Danger!"

The photographer looked over his shoulder in time to see the stricken airplane shift in its straps. It began to fall in slow motion back toward the bottom. Eyes wide, the man looked back at Mike and then took off swimming as hard as he could directly away from the danger zone. His anger at Mike for dragging him away immediately forgotten. Mike followed behind him another 20 feet and then turned to watch the plane crash to the bottom for the second time.

Still tied to the other lift bags, although two of them came loose under the sudden strain of the shifting load and the additional weight from the loss of the one bag, the plane rolled in the water and landed back on the reef on its side this time with the opening where the missing wing had been crashing into the bottom first. Landing diagonally on the reef caused the fuselage to buckle and collapse. The weight of the still-attached left wing drove the aluminum shell into the bottom destroying the main cabin, and with it much of the evidence of the crash. It would take investigators months to reconstruct the plane in an airport hangar now.

CHAPTER EIGHT

Mike swam slowly back toward the dive boat. Through his quick actions the local underwater photographer escaped with nothing more than a bruised ego. Once he was sure everyone was clear, Mike picked his camera up from the ocean bottom before he returned to the boat. He was lost in thought, trying to get a handle on everything that had happened in the last 24 hours. It wasn't his first close scrape or the first time he faced the possibility of death. It wasn't even the first time this year. But it most certainly was the first time that he almost died twice from the same plane crash. Mike didn't believe in coincidences and this whole mess was getting stranger and stranger. It would be up to the professionals to determine exactly what happened, but Mike was sure a bomb had been detonated in the fuselage of the plane to bring it down. And what was the story with the Arabic script he saw inside? One thing was for sure, while Mike knew he wasn't targeted by whoever caused the plane to crash, it had nearly landed on him twice. That made him mad. And when he got mad, he got to the bottom of whatever was going on.

As Mike approached the stern of the dive boat to make his exit, he noticed a crowd waiting for him. And then it dawned on him that everyone on every other dive boat was watching him as well. And they were cheering. Loudly. He had been so deep into his thoughts he hadn't even heard them. Everyone in the water saw what Mike did to save one of their own and they told everyone else. They weren't going to let Mike's efforts go unrecognized.

Captain Lynn was waiting for Mike at the swim step and took Mike's camera, mask and fins from him as he climbed the ladder out of the water. Other hands reached out and removed Mike's scuba unit from him. As soon as he was free of his gear, dozens of hands reached out to shake his or to pat him on the back with well-wishes.

"Good on ya!"

"Masha danki ruman hombe!"

"Way to go!"

"Bon salud!"

The coast guard and police quickly took control of the scene and announced over the radio that the diving was done for the day. Any evidence collected should be delivered to the police dock, along with original copies of all photographs, but because of the accident and the potential further damage to the plane, they were going to explore other options to bring the plane to the surface. With the bodies recovered and initial photographs taken, there was less urgency. It might be a week or more before the wreckage was recovered.

Once the dive boat got underway, and the other divers had given Mike a few minutes to himself — after many promises that he would not be buying his own drinks any time soon — Mike moved forward to talk to Lynn.

"Certainly been an interesting couple days," Mike said. He moved into the pilot's area and leaned against a bulkhead so he could roll with the motion of the boat, but still be close enough to hear what she said.

"You've got that right, Mike. I've never seen anything like this."

"Do you know anything about the commercial divers who were handling the actual lift? Where did they come from?"

"I heard they work for the oil refinery in Willemstad. I don't know them, though. It's a small island, but they don't mix with the recreational divers and the tourist crowd."

"So, their normal job is maintaining the refinery facilities where they load refined gas and unload crude oil and that sort of thing?"

"Guess so, yeah."

"I'm sure they are all trained and certified as commercial divers. It's really strange that a lift bag would fail like that."

"I've never seen it either. The thing shot 20 feet into the air when it broke free. Came out of the water like a missile. I pulled it out of the water when it landed."

"You grabbed the lift bag? Do you still have it?"

"Yeah, it's right behind you in the cargo hold. I figured the police would want to look at it. Those commercial divers called over the radio asking if anyone had seen it. They said they wanted to get it back. Before I got a chance to tell them I had it, you got to the surface and everyone was cheering. I figured they could wait a little while to get their bag back."

Mike listened to Lynn with one ear while he moved forward to the cargo hold and grabbed the now-deflated lift bag. He had used them from time to time. They were pretty simple devices, really. The commercial grade versions, like this one, had a fill valve on the bottom that a diver would use to the add air to the bag. It was made from a vulcanized rubber material reinforced with Kevlar. Straps attached to the bag from the top to the bottom extended below the bag so they could be attached to whatever was being lifted. Mike looked the bag over closely, but he stopped when he got to the straps hanging below the bag. One of them had been cut about two-thirds of the way across. The weight of the lift had ripped the belt the rest of the way, but by that time, whoever had cut the belt had moved to another location. Mike recalled that the four commercial divers were circulating from bag to bag to make sure everything was going as planned. None of the recreational divers got close enough to the lift bags to sabotage them, or at least not that Mike saw, but he wasn't watching them every minute, either.

One thing was for certain, someone sabotaged the lift. Whoever was doing all this wanted to make sure the plane wasn't recovered any time soon. The authorities would bring it to the surface eventually. There was no way to avoid that. But the lift accident had definitely slowed things down. The question was *Why? What did it serve? And why sabotage the plane in the first place? Was it terror? That didn't make a lot of sense. Downing a private plane wouldn't terrorize the world as much as a commercial airliner. No, something else was going on here.*

CHAPTER NINE

Back in his hotel in Willemstad, Mike downloaded the images from his digital camera and selected the best ones to send to his editor at *First Account* magazine. He wrote up a quick account of what he saw, including the plane crashing back down onto the reef. He wrestled for a few minutes about whether to include his suspicion that the lift bag had been cut, but finally did mention it, along with including a photo of the lift bag itself. He knew his editor would have reporters chasing down information on their end. He hadn't heard, but wouldn't be surprised if a reporter was on a plane to Curacao to cover the story from the local angle. A small plane crash was a big deal for the national news in the United States, and now that it was likely it had been sabotaged the story would get bigger. Of course, he just happened to be there so his editor was going to take full advantage of the story.

Before Mike closed his computer, he sent one of his photos of the Arabic script he saw inside the fuselage to a friend. Mike had worked in the Middle East on several occasions and understood enough of the languages of the region to get around, but reading it was an entire different story. His friend, Amal, had been his interpreter in Afghanistan and he trusted the man without question. Something about the Arabic message didn't add up, so Mike wanted to know what it said.

His work done, Mike moved out onto his hotel balcony and thought about what he saw inside the plane. His mind went back to the letter he saw in the top of the briefcase. He had a photo of the letter and the case where it was stuffed under one of the luxury seats in the main cabin. It was addressed to President Arturo of Venezuela. Since there was only one passenger, the briefcase had to belong to him; Ryan Stone. Mike had learned he worked for an oil company. He knew he could check the pilot's flight plan, and was sure someone already had, but that would only tell him what airport they were heading to. Stone must have been meeting with the President. That was the only reason Mike could think of for Stone to have that letter. It was an introduction of some sort. Considering what happened to the plane just a few minutes later, Mike wished he had tampered with evidence and pulled the briefcase down and looked at the rest of the letter. Now there was no way of knowing how long it would take for investigators to get back inside the plane and make sense of everything. The odds that they would even pay attention to the man's briefcase in the next few months were slim. They would be looking for cause of the crash, not the motive for the sabotage.

The oil industry around the world was in crisis at the moment. The OPEC nations couldn't agree on restricting production and there was a glut of oil on the market. It was keeping gas prices low, which was a boon for the average citizen, but crippling for the industries that were laying off employees by the thousands and for the governments that were losing billions in tax revenue. Venezuela was one of the hardest hit. Their national economy was based almost exclusively on oil and with oil prices at record lows, the nation was a disaster. There were food shortages and protests. Insert Stone's visit and possible meeting with President Arturo and then the plane crash into the middle of it and suddenly the word conspiracy wasn't far from Mike's mind. *But who? And what were they up to?*

Mike remembered his determination to talk to the pilot. The second crash of the jet plane had distracted him from that idea for a bit. Mike thought the pilot might have an idea what was going on. She was alive and still in the local hospital. If nothing else, Mike wanted to check on her and make sure she was doing all right. Mike thought back to the satellite phone that he saw off the hook in the downed plane. She might know if Stone had made a call as well and who it was to. Of course, she might not know anything about her passenger and the phone could have simply been knocked loose from where it rested during the crash, but it never hurt to ask the question.

CHAPTER TEN

Mike walked into St. Elizabeth's Hospital in Willemstad and quickly got his bearings. It was an island hospital, but a well-organized and busy one. It was also the Dutch hospital, built by the former government before giving Curacao its independence. It covered everything from delivering babies to trauma. There was a smaller "international" hospital on the island, but that was mostly geared toward visitors to the island who got sick. Mike was sure the authorities would bring the pilot to St. Elizabeth. The pilot's name tag read Anderson, Mike remembered. He had scanned the local press and online news reports about the crash, but hadn't found out anything more about the pilot.

Mike knew he was going to have to talk his way in to meet her. Hospitals weren't in the business of giving up patient information to strangers. He thought about acting like he was family, but without her first name, that would be tricky…if not impossible. He had two other options. He could flash his press ID or he could simply tell the person at the front desk the truth. At least to a point.

"Hi, my name is Mike. I'm looking to check on a patient in the hospital and I'm hoping you can help me. I don't actually know her first name or what room she's in," Mike began.

"Are you are family member?" the matronly woman behind the counter asked, barely looking up from her paperwork.

"Well, no, I'm not."

"Then, I'm sorry I can't help you. I can't give out patient information unless you are immediate family."

"I understand that and I hate to even ask. I know someone like you must get all sorts of ridiculous requests and I know people can be rude. I'm not like that, I promise. But, you see, I pulled her from the water yesterday and I just wanted to make sure she was all right." Mike smiled his best smile.

"You mean the pilot lady from the awful plane crash?"

"That's the one. I was on the dive boat that almost got hit by the plane. We jumped in the water and pulled her to safety. I just want to make sure she's doing okay."

"I guess it can't hurt for you to see her. You saved her life after all." The woman turned to her computer and began looking up the information.

"You're too kind. I was just doing what I could to help. Nothing more than anyone else would have done in the situation." Mike continued to pour on the charm and give her his best "aww-shucks" smile.

"Her name is Carol Anderson and she is in room 311, but you better hurry. She's being released today. At least from the hospital. I'm sure the authorities are gonna ask her to stay around for a while for the investigation." The woman took on a conspiratorial tone.

"I'm sure you're right about that. Thanks for the information. You've been a great help!"

Mike made his way through the hospital, looking for the room. Getting off the elevator on the third floor, Mike was struck by how similar hospitals were all over the world. He had recently spent some time in the hospital in George Town, Grand Cayman himself after a crazy hacker trying to rob international banks shot him. If his friend Rich and his girlfriend Frankie hadn't been there, he might not have made it. Of course, the chest wound had kept him out of the water for several months while he healed. He had taken the time to give some guest lectures and work on his latest book. He had finally gotten cleared to return to work, and to dive again, but the sights, sounds and smells of the hospital brought it all back to him. It wasn't an experience he wanted to repeat.

Something seemed out of place for Mike as he walked down the corridor to Carol's room. Over the years he had met a number of characters who operated on all sides of the law and more than one who worked for international intelligence agencies, the one in Langley, Virginia and for other nations. Over beers and cigars in dingy dive bars in international backwaters, Mike learned a few things about what they referred to as "trade craft". While very few people in the CIA, or any other agency, were spies in the Hollywood sense of the word, there were people operating in treacherous circumstances where blending in, or noticing others who were trying not to be noticed, was a matter of life and death.

Mike slowed down a step, calmed his breathing and opened his senses to his surroundings. He put his own thoughts and memories about his time in the hospital away to focus on the here and now. Nearly everything looked normal. But not everything. There were two men loitering in the hall. One looked vaguely like a doctor, with a white lab coat on, but Mike couldn't see any sign of a hospital ID. Another man was sitting in a chair in the hallway, holding a magazine like he was reading it. Except he wasn't.

Both men were watching the hall and everyone in it. They looked Mediterranean or Middle Eastern.

He finally reached the room he was looking for, 311, so he filed his unease away for the moment. Looking in, Mike couldn't see anyone. Was he too late? Had she already checked out? No, there was a bag on the bed. He stepped into the room just as the door to the bathroom opened and Carol stepped out.

"Oh, Hi. You startled me," Carol said, coming face to face with Mike. "Are you here to wheel me downstairs?"

Mike had only gotten a brief look at the woman when they pulled her from the water and then gave her CPR. He hadn't really taken the time to notice her appearance. Just that she was breathing. Carol stood nearly six feet tall, with her blond hair pulled back in a ponytail. She wasn't wearing any makeup, but was still pretty. She appeared fit, like a distance runner, and about 40 years old. She was wearing a polo shirt and had long tanned legs showing below her shorts.

"I'll be happy to do that for you, but no, that's not why I'm here," Mike said with a shake of his head. He thought for just a moment about letting her think that he worked at the hospital, but then he would have to change his story when they got to the front door. His sense that something was going on was growing by the second and he needed her to trust him.

"Oh, um, are you a doctor? Or one of the investigators? I'm sorry, the last 24 hours has been a blur and I am still trying to process it all. Have we met? So many people have been in and out of here, we could have met five minutes ago and I'm not sure I would remember."

Mike laughed at that question.

"Yes, and no. I was on the dive boat on the reef where you crashed. I was there when we pulled you from the water and gave you CPR."

"Oh! Wow," Carol sat down on the edge of the hospital bed. "I, I, just wow. You saved my life. Thank you for that."

"I'm just glad we were there to help you. My name is Mike, by the way."

"Just before we hit the water, everything was going in slow motion. My co-pilot and I were doing everything we could to get the plane under control, but nothing was working. I actually remember seeing a boat on the water for a brief second and then we hit. All I remember is the water after that."

"I'm sure the whole thing has been traumatic for you. I assume they'll want you to talk to doctors and therapists for a while before you fly again. I'm a little surprised they are releasing you from the hospital already to be honest."

"That's a little strange now that you mention it. Yesterday they were talking about me being here for several days and then a new doctor came in this morning and told me they were releasing me. I'm physically fine, so there's no reason for me to stay here, but it did seem a little strange."

"If for no other reason to monitor you for the effects of almost drowning or concussion."

"That's what I thought, too."

"So, where do you go from here?"

"Everything I had, including money and my clothes is in the wreckage of the plane. The local Red Cross gave me these clothes and some toiletry things. They gave me a voucher for a hotel room, too, but the air charter company I work for has set me up with a room at a local hotel. They sent me a telegram to say they were wiring me some money, too. Someone from the company is on the way to take charge of our side of the investigation."

"I know the island pretty well and I have a car. If you want, I'll be happy to take you where you need to go. There's a great little cafe not far from here if you want to get some lunch. It sure beats hospital food. And they have ice-cold Amstel."

Before Carol had a chance to answer, the man Mike saw in the hall came into her room. He was still wearing his white lab coat, but Mike still couldn't see any sign of identification.

"Miss Anderson, I've come to take you to your hotel room. Your company has arranged everything," the man said in heavily-accented English.

"That won't be necessary. Mike here is a friend. He has offered to help me out."

"But Miss Anderson, I have orders…"

"I heard you, but I can take care of myself. Thank you," she said, ending the last forcefully.

"I don't think you understand," the man said, reaching out to grab Carol's arm. Before he touched her, Mike stepped forward, placing himself in front of the man.

"I don't think you understand," Mike replied. "I'll help Carol out. You aren't needed." Mike stood directly in front of the mystery man, and looked down at him. Mike was six inches taller and at least 40 pounds heavier. Able to get close to the man for the first time, Mike confirmed his suspicion that the man was from the Middle East. He wondered if the man would press it any further and cause a scene, but the mystery man took a step backward and readdressed himself to Carol.

"I see you have made up your mind. I believe you are making a mistake. I will let your employer know." Without another word, the man turned and left the hospital room.

"Well, that was interesting," Carol said.

"I appreciate you trusting me, but what made you make the decision?" Mike asked.

"I don't know exactly. I travel a lot for my job and I've developed a pretty good sense about the people I meet. It's not failed me yet. He put me off from the moment he stepped into the room. He just seemed creepy."

"And what did your sense say about me?"

"Well, you did save my life so I owe you that much trust. And a cold Amstel sounds lovely right now."

#####

Mike took Carol straight to a small waterfront cafe where they could relax and talk. There were more commercial or tourist-friendly places than the one Mike chose, but like Carol's sense, Mike's was telling him something was going on and he was worried about Carol's safety. Aside from that, he preferred places where you might see locals, rather than visitors.

"That's a really unique bridge," Carol said looking out on the waterway. "It's flat. How do ships get in and out here? I know the refinery is that way," she said with a gesture toward the interior of the island.

Carol referred to the Queen Emma Bridge that crossed St. Anna Bay and connected the Punda and Otrobanda sections of Willemstad. It was a pontoon bridge. Diesel engines drove propellers which moved the bridge to allow boat traffic to pass.

"You're right, it is. It actually rotates out of the way like a swing arm. I'm sure we'll see it open up before long. There's quite a bit of boat traffic in and out of the harbor. When it's open, there are ferries you can take across to the other side. Or you wait."

"Interesting bit of engineering. Now, about that beer," Carol said with a smile. Mike could tell she was relaxing now that she was away from the hospital and could feel the fresh breeze on her face. They quickly ordered and Mike sat quietly for a minute. The server returned in a moment with two Amstel Brights in small cans.

"What's the story with these?" Carol asked after taking a long drink and nearly emptying the can.

"It's stays pretty hot here, year-round. They serve the beer in these small cans so it doesn't have a chance to get warm on you." Mike signaled their server to bring two more beers out for them.

"Okay, Mike, you do certainly seem to know your way around this island. So, why don't you tell me what's going on here. I think you know more than you've told me so far."

"Okay, first, I really was there when we pulled you out of the water and I gave you CPR. But, I am also a journalist. I'm a photographer for *First Account* Magazine."

"Please tell me you're not some newsie trying to get close to me for a story."

"No, I'm not. I would have come to check on you anyway, but there's something going on and I want to figure it out. I was hoping to ask you some questions about your trip and where you were heading."

"What do you mean 'something going on'?" Carol made air quotes with her fingers.

"To begin with, your plane crash wasn't an accident." Mike quickly caught Carol up on everything he saw on the dive to recover the plane while they ate, including the sabotage so the plane wouldn't be recovered. At least not yet. Mike knew they would eventually get the plane off the bottom and the investigators would tear it apart. That told him whoever orchestrated all of this wanted to delay things just a little bit longer. Whatever those *things* were.

"Honestly, I don't know that much about what our passenger was up to. He was pretty typical of our charters. We get a final destination and we get there, but we don't spend a lot of time talking. He was nice enough, but he looked like he was pretty preoccupied when he got on the plane."

"I'm guessing your final destination was Caracas, right? You weren't heading here."

"Yes, that's right. I don't know who Mr. Stone was meeting with, but he did have some authority. We were told we had priority approach when we got close. They were going to direct us right into the General Aviation area and get us on the ground. The plan was that Mr. Stone would be met plane-side and taken off to his meeting."

"He wasn't going to have to clear Customs or anything? That tells me whoever he was meeting with was pretty high up and would make sense with the letter in his briefcase addressed to the President of Venezuela."

"I'm sorry, Mike, but I really don't know any more than that. And we were so busy in the last few minutes before we went down that I barely had a chance to see the island in front of us. I sure didn't get to talk to Mr. Stone before we went down."

"Do you know if he made a phone call just before you crashed?"

"Now that you mention it, I do remember seeing the indicator light flip on. It lets us know when there is an outgoing signal on the satellite phone."

"Is there any way to know who he called?"

"Every outgoing call is logged into the computer on board the plane. It's backed up on the satellite network as well, but I don't have any way of getting to that."

"You've been great, Carol. Thank you. I know you've been through a lot and you're probably exhausted. I'll run you to your hotel so you can get some more rest. If you need anything, don't hesitate to call me. I'll be happy to do whatever I can."

As Mike stood up, he stretched and looked around at the quiet street. Immediately, a siren began sounding in his head. The second Middle Eastern man Mike saw in the hospital hallway near Carol's room was sitting at a table in a nearby cafe 50 feet away from them. There was no way this was a coincidence. The man was sipping coffee and acting disinterested in his surroundings, but that would be exactly how he would want to look. First the pushy "doctor" in the hospital and now this man. Someone was following Carol, but for what reason. Was she in danger? And what could he do about it?

CHAPTER ELEVEN

The last thing Mike wanted to do was alarm Carol. She had certainly been through enough in the last 24 hours and he knew she hadn't really even begun to process it all. When she spoke about the crash and the aftermath, she never mentioned her co-pilot. Even if they weren't friends, a man she worked with had died right beside her. That would leave a mark on anyone. He knew it was all going to come rushing back soon. He just hoped whatever was going on, whoever was watching her, was gone by then.

Mike pulled his rental car into a parking space in front of the hotel and shut the ignition off to go inside. He didn't know anything about the hotel, but it looked respectable enough. The charter plane company made the reservation for Carol and should have picked up the tab. Mike began to open his door when Carol stopped him.

"Mike, there's no need for you to come inside. I'll be okay."

"I just want to make sure everything is set up. You don't have a credit card in case they ask for one for "incidentals" like every hotel in the world."

While that much was true, Mike also wanted to check things out and make sure there weren't any more sinister surprises waiting for Carol inside. Mike stood by while Carol checked in at the front desk. Everything had been arranged by the charter company and they had even wired her a few hundred dollars just in case she needed something.

The front desk clerk finished up and handed her the card key. "Ma'am, you'll be in room 419. If you need anything, don't hesitate to ask. The elevator is right behind you."

"Thank you." Carol turned to Mike.

"Just take care of yourself and let me know if you need anything else. You have my number. It's my cell phone and it works here on the island. I will be around a few more days before I head off to my next assignment. If you want to get some dinner or another little beer, let me know."

"Thank you, Mike." She gave him a quick hug and headed for the elevator. Mike watched her walk across the lobby and then scanned the room for anything out of place. Nothing made his gut churn. Mike debated letting hotel security know, but when he thought about it he realized how ridiculous that conversation would be. What would he tell them? That a couple creepy guys made him uncomfortable? He knew that conversation was a nonstarter. He would just have to figure out what was going on before anything else happened.

When Mike got to his rental car, he unlocked the door and immediately saw the backpack the Red Cross had given Carol with the toiletries and a change of clothes. He knew she had some money to go shopping, but he was also confident she was going to want something fresh to change into in the morning. Mike grabbed the pack and headed back into the hotel. He remembered hearing the room she had been assigned to. 419. "Funny. In the US, they never say the room number out loud at the front desk," Mike said to himself as he got on the elevator. "They don't want anyone to be able to follow you."

Getting off the elevator, Mike immediately knew something was wrong. Everything looked normal, but that feeling in the pit of his stomach was suddenly back. He glanced at the room numbers on the wall and saw Carol's room was down the hall to his right. Moving quickly down the hallway, Mike spotted room 419 and could tell the door was ajar. He moved up as quietly as he could and listened for a moment. The door was blocked open by the reinforcing latch. It had been flipped into the door jamb intentionally.

"Carol, are you in there? I brought you your backpack. You left it in my car." Silence.

Maybe she stepped back out for ice and didn't want to take her key.

Mike looked around the hallway, trying to figure out where the ice machine was so he could check. "Carol. Are you in there?" Mike pushed gently on the door. As he did, a hand reached out and grabbed Mike's arm, dragging him into the room.

#####

Half expecting something to happen, Mike reacted to the pull on his arm in a way his attacker didn't expect. He pushed forward instead of pulling back and slammed his attacker against the wall with the door. Mike was rewarded with an "Oof" as he knocked the breath from the man's lungs.

Barreling into the room, Mike sized up the situation. A second man was holding Carol in the middle of the room with his hand over her mouth to keep her quiet. Both men were wearing ski masks to hide their faces. Mike couldn't tell if the man holding Carol had a gun on her or not. He hesitated for a moment, concerned the man might kill her.

Seeing Mike and realizing she had backup, Carol jammed her foot down on her attacker's instep like she had been taught in a self-defense class. When he relaxed his grip on her arms, Carol jammed her elbow into the man's stomach. When he bent over from the blow, Carol broke free and brought her knee into the man's groin, dropping him to the ground.

"Come on!" Mike shouted and turned for the door. The first man had regained his feet and was drawing a gun from the holster on his belt. Mike swung Carol's backpack at the man and knocked his arm down, sending the gun out of his grip and onto the floor. The man reached for the gun and as he did Mike grabbed the man's head and forced it down while he brought his knee up into the man's nose. Mike heard a crack and the man's knees buckled, sending him to the floor. Carol grabbed the pistol, a semi-automatic Glock, from the floor and followed Mike out the door.

"Which way?" Carol asked when the made it out of the room.

"I don't know if there are any more of them, but we have to assume there are."

Mike ran to the elevator and punched both the Up and Down buttons and then said "Down the back stairs!"

They made it down the four flights of stairs and out of the hotel without seeing anyone else. Mike's car was parked in front of the hotel. When they got outside, Mike motioned for Carol to wait while he looked things over. He handed her the backpack and she tucked the gun inside the bag.

Mike crept between cars in the parking lot and worked his way toward his rental car. He was almost there when two men burst through the front door of the hotel. Mike hadn't had a chance to notice what the two men were wearing when they were in the room. Neither man was wearing a ski mask, but one man's nose was obviously broken and bleeding. He was sure it was the two men that had jumped them. Mike hid behind a car to watch them for a second. He needed to know if they were on their own, or if they had help.

The two men looked around the parking lot trying to find Mike and Carol. And then Mike saw what he needed to know, but exactly what he didn't want to see. The man with the broken nose raised his arm to signal to someone across the parking lot. A car started moving across the parking lot. Mike's stomach dropped when he saw it was a police car.

"Well, that sucks," Mike muttered.

#####

Mike made his way back to where Carol was hiding and quickly caught her up on what he saw.

"So the police are against us, too?" Carol asked.

"Honestly, I doubt it. At least not all of them. It's probably just one or two."

"But we can't be sure who is involved in this and who isn't."

"We're on our own, at least for now."

"Exactly what is *this* anyway? What's going on? Why were those men trying to grab me?"

"I have no idea. For the moment, let's figure a way out of here and then we'll work on the bigger picture. Agreed?"

"Agreed."

Mike surveyed the hotel parking lot for possibilities. They needed to find a way out. The front parking lot was full of rental cars and newer vehicles. Not much help, there. He could just see the police car at the opening to the parking lot. It looked like whoever was behind the wheel was making sure no one got out that way. Mike could see one of the two men from in the hotel slowly walking between cars as well. He was moving slowly, going row by row, looking for his quarry. Mike couldn't see the second man, but he knew he wouldn't be far away. They weren't going to get that lucky.

Since leaving by the front wasn't going to work, Mike looked around the back lot. And then his eyes landed on exactly what they needed. In what was obviously the employee lot, Mike saw an early 1980s model Jeep CJ-7. The owner had removed the doors and only had a bikini top for the roof. Mike could tell the Jeep had seen better days, that didn't matter at the moment. There wouldn't be any problem getting inside and the old Jeep had a simple ignition that Mike knew he could hotwire.

Mike motioned to Carol to meet him at the Jeep as he began moving that direction. Over the years he had owned and driven a number of Jeep CJs and Wranglers. He never cared for the bigger Grand Cherokee, always opting for the smaller wheelbase vehicles. They reached the old Jeep at the same time and Mike was pleased with what he saw. Carol was less impressed.

"What are we going to do with this thing?"

"This will be our magic carpet ride out of here. Climb in the back and cover yourself up with that blanket. This'll just take a minute."

Mike sat up in the driver's seat and pushed in the clutch while he twisted some of the loose wires together. He was instantly rewarded with the familiar click of the ignition relay engaging accompanied by the red glow of the low oil pressure warning light. Finally, Mike identified the starter wire, stripped back about half an inch of the insulation with the pocket knife he always kept with him to expose the copper within. He quickly wrapped the entire length of the starter wire around his finger a few turns to form a spring-like coil. With just a slight extension of the wire, Mike was able to bring the starter wire close enough to the ignition bundle to generate a fairly generous spark followed immediately by the sound of the engine turning over. In that brief moment, in what seemed like an eternity, the sound of "whir, whir, whir" was drowned out by the sound of the old Jeep roaring to life. Mike let go of the starter wire and it sprung back into its shortened form a bit like a turtle pulling its head back into its shell. That done, Mike was able to quickly move on to the next task at hand. Carol was lying down in the floor where the back seat would normally be. Mike gave her a nod and she pulled an old blanket over her. Mike took off his shirt and pulled a ball cap off of the rear view mirror where the owner left it hanging. That was the only way to quickly change his appearance on the fly. He pulled the hat down over his head as far as it would go. He eased the Jeep into reverse and backed out of the parking space.

Mike did his best to move slowly and deliberately. He knew if he suddenly raced out of the parking lot, it would attract attention. As he shifted the Jeep into first gear he saw the second man scanning the building and the parking lot. This was the man with the broken nose. Mike knew there was no way the man had gotten a good look at him. From a quick glance, Mike could see the man's eyes were turning black and his nose was swollen. There was still blood on his face. Mike doubted the man could even see clearly, all things considered. If he just stayed cool, Mike was confident he could slip past the man and they could get away. He began moving toward the back exit of the parking lot and switched on the radio to complete his disguise as a hotel employee getting off work for the day.

"Hey! That's my Jeep. Come back here!"

Mike glanced around to see a young man come running out of the hotel's back door yelling and waving at him. That was the one thing he hadn't planned on. He had been so focused on avoiding Carol's captors, he hadn't given a thought to the actual owner of the Jeep. Mike hit the accelerator pedal and was rewarded with a throaty growl as the old Jeep's engine roared. Mike smiled knowing the owner had taken good care of the engine if not the body. In the back of his mind, Mike swore to himself that he would make it up to the young man.

"I just hope the other guy ignores me, thinking it's just a car theft," Mike said to himself as he wheeled the Jeep around the corner. He had a straight shot for the exit and the road leading away from the hotel.

A moment later, Mike got his answer when he heard three gun shots split the air. One bullet hit the Jeep's windshield, spiderwebbing the passenger side. Mike shifted into second gear and felt the Jeep leap forward. This just got serious. They were still 20 feet away from the exit when Mike saw the police car accelerating directly toward him. It came sliding to a stop directly in front of him, blocking the exit. The driver opened his door and began drawing a gun as well. Out of the corner of his eye, Mike saw the other man from inside the hotel running toward them from where he was searching the front parking area. They were about to be trapped in a three-way shoot out and the odds on either of them surviving were non-existent. Mike was sure it would all be covered up as a car-jacking gone wrong and he and Carol's bodies would simply disappear, another problem resolved.

There was only one choice left. Mike hoped the Jeep's owner had taken as good of care of the suspension as he had of the engine. Mike grabbed third gear and accelerated directly at the police car. The man fired a wild shot and then dove back inside his cruiser for safety. He thought Mike was going to crash directly into him.

"Hold on!" he shouted to Carol. He knew she was about to get bounced around pretty hard.

At the last moment, Mike swerved to the side and bounced over the curb and the landscaping that made up the outside of the parking lot. The Jeep bounced into the air and the engine roared as the wheels left the ground. As soon as they hit the main road, Mike downshifted and fought to get the vehicle under control. They bounced twice and then Mike was able to steer. He shot off down the road. In his rearview mirror, Mike saw the two men jump into the police car with the driver and then they worked to get turned around. This wasn't over yet.

"Are you okay" Mike shouted over his shoulder.

Carol flung the blanket away and began climbing into the front passenger seat. She started to scold Mike and then was stopped cold by the sight of the bullet hole and the shattered glass in front of her.

"What are you? Some sort of action hero or something?"

"Mostly the 'or something' part." Mike caught her up with what had happened since she covered herself up with the blanket.

"Are you able to outrun them?"

"Doubtful. We aren't geared for top-end speed. And you can never outrun a radio. We have to assume they are working with someone else and can call ahead. We may be swarmed by police cars any minute."

"So we need to ditch this thing and find a place to hide."

"Exactly."

CHAPTER TWELVE

Mike raced away from the hotel as quickly as he could. There was no need to be subtle now. For a moment, Mike thought about heading into the middle of the island, toward the oil refinery, thinking there would be good places to ditch the Jeep, but then he realized they would be stuck without transportation or communication with the outside world. At an intersection, he turned back toward town and quickly found a quiet alley a few blocks away from the touristy parts of Willemstad. They hadn't seen any signs of pursuit, but Mike was sure they would be coming for them. Getting away from someone chasing you on an island was a temporary thing. There was only so far you could run.

Willemstad was first established in 1634 when the Dutch captured the island from Spain. The colonial powers that designed the city originally brought what they knew about architecture and city planning with them from western Europe. The city was filled with small alleys and blind turns that wouldn't make sense in the modern car culture. But that worked out perfectly for Mike and Carol. Mike tucked the Jeep in behind a dumpster and grabbed his shirt off of the floorboard. He tossed the owner's hat back over the rearview mirror and got out. He patted the Jeep's hood and thanked the machine for getting them out of a tight spot and again reminded himself that he would make it up to the owner. He hoped. If he didn't get out of this mess, there wasn't much he was going to be able to do.

"So what do we do now?" Carol asked.

"Let's find another cafe or locals diner and get off the streets. We need to regroup and make a plan."

They found themselves walking along a side waterway that connected to St. Anna Bay. There were fishing boats tied up selling their fresh catch to the local restaurants and an open air farmer's market full of produce. Mike remembered a place that would be perfect for them to catch their breath for a while as they figured out their next steps. In just another moment, he found it. It was an open-air restaurant with picnic tables packed closely inside the structure. Four women stood behind the counter fixing an endless stream of fish stews, fried fish and vegetables. There was a constant stream of people coming and going, picking up an evening meal to take home after work and or eating there. Mike knew no one would pay any attention to them, as long as they ordered food. They got in line and grabbed themselves a selection of local cuisine and then headed to a table off to one side.

"Now what do we do?" Carol asked.

"Well, first you eat."

"I'm not really hungry…"

"It really wasn't a suggestion. We aren't out of the woods yet and we're going to need all of our strength."

Carol glared at Mike for a moment, but didn't say anything. She picked up her fork and put a bite in her mouth. Mike knew she was simply stressed and overwhelmed with everything that had happened from the plane crash to the attempted abduction to being shot at and bounced around in the Jeep. He didn't take her anger personally.

"There are a few things you don't know about." He quickly caught her up on seeing the two Middle Eastern men in the hospital.

"So, that's why you were so insistent with the doctor who came in as we were leaving."

"I don't think he was actually a doctor."

"He was going to try to kidnap me directly from the hospital?"

"It sure seemed that way."

"So this is some sort of Middle Eastern terror plot?"

"That's the weird part. The men in the hotel were white and the man in the police car was black. He wasn't wearing a uniform, by the way, so I'm not sure if he was a cop or not."

"They could be mercenaries or something."

"That's very true, but I think we are missing something here."

"Yeah, like why they're coming after me."

Before Mike could respond, he heard a chime from his phone. It was an email. He hadn't even thought to look at it since everything had happened. He pulled up the email application and looked at the top message. It was a response to the email he sent with the picture of the Arabic script from his friend in Afghanistan.

"What is it?"

"When I made a dive on the plane this morning, there was a message written in Arabic inside the fuselage where the bomb was placed. I sent a picture of it to a friend of mine to ask what it said. He just replied to say it just said 'Allahu Akbar.' That means 'God is great.'"

"That's something terrorists say isn't it?"

"Yes, they do. But it's also a basic greeting and blessing in Islam. It's not much of a message."

"What's this all about Mike?"

"I wish I knew the answer to that question. Like I said, there's something going on here and we don't have the full story."

"Which brings me back to my original question."

"First, I'm going to send an email to my editor and get her help. She can find a *fixer* here on the island that can protect us."

"What's a *fixer*?"

"Someone local who is well-connected. They handle transportation, security and that sort of thing."

"Have you used *fixers* before?"

"Well, not on an island like Curacao, but yes in other places. My job takes me places where personal safety is sometimes a little tenuous. It helps to have someone who knows how to get around."

"And you trust these people?"

"Most don't really care who they work for, as long as they're paid in advance. Most of the time, you don't really have a choice, but I've never had one betray me, if that's what you're asking."

"So, we just stay here until the fixer arrives?"

"No, this place will close down in a little while. The sun is setting and most of the locals will be home soon. It's already starting to clear out. We need to find a place to hide. Do you still have that hotel voucher from the Red Cross?"

"It's here in the backpack they gave me."

"With that we should be able to check into the hotel without using a credit card. I don't know who these people are, but I'm guessing they have the means to check for a digital signature and track us that way."

"I have a couple hundred bucks the charter company wired to me, too."

"Good. I have some cash as well. We stay off the grid and wait for the cavalry to arrive."

Mike looked at Carol's plate and realized it was completely empty and smiled. "I'm glad to see you weren't hungry."

"I guess I was hungrier than I thought." She grinned. "Mike, thank you. I don't know why you're helping me, but I would be dead by now if it weren't for you."

"I don't like to be shot at, either. Let's go."

They left the diner and started heading back toward the hospital. They didn't know exactly where the hotel was, but knew it was close by. They never made it.

CHAPTER THIRTEEN

Out of the corner of his eye, Mike could just see what was going on. And he didn't like it. He did a mental survey of his own body and didn't think anything was broken, but he couldn't move his arms or his legs. From the way he was sitting, he guessed he was tied to a chair with his hands behind his back. There was duct tape over his mouth so he couldn't talk or scream. Mike did his best to keep his head still and keep his eyes mostly closed so no one would realize he was awake yet. He needed to find out what was going on.

In front of him, Mike saw five men. He recognized three from the hotel, but he had never seen the other two before. As Mike's eyes cleared and he was able to focus, he realized Carol was in the same situation as he was. Except she was in trouble. She faced his direction, about 20 feet away from him, but she wasn't looking at Mike. One of the two new men was in her face, grilling her for answers and threatening her. Mike guessed the man was in charge of the group. The other four men seemed to defer to him. None of the men, four white and one black, but none Arabic, were attempting to hide their appearance. That fact was telling and troubling at the same time.

"Tell me what you know!" the boss screamed at Carol.

"I'll tell you anything, but I don't know what you want. I don't know anything…" Carol was on the verge of tears and seemed only semi-conscious. She had bruises on her face and a bloody lip. The Boss' interrogation style obviously included pain.

"What did Stone tell you about his trip? Did he tell you what he was going to do?"

"No, he was just a passenger. He was nice enough, but we didn't really talk. He seemed distracted when he got on board, like he had things on his mind."

"I don't believe you," the boss growled in her face.

"It's the truth, I swear. We were just taking him to Venezuela. He didn't tell us why." Carol began to sob.

After a moment, and without warning, the Boss slapped Carol hard with his open hand. She nearly fell over, but one of the other men grabbed her chair and straightened her up.

"Now listen to me. The pain can stop. All you have to do is answer my questions. Who did Stone call from the plane?"

"I don't know!" Carol shouted. "I told you that already. We were trying to save the plane. I didn't pay attention to the phone number the man dialed. We were in crisis mode. I wouldn't have looked anyway, but right then it was the last thing I cared about."

One of the other men stepped up to talk to the Boss.

"I think she's telling the truth."

"I agree, but I had to make sure. That's what they paid us to do. There weren't supposed to be any loose ends after the plane crash. When she lived, we had to make sure she didn't know anything. If she did, she could have told someone and that would be even more trouble."

"What's this all about anyway?"

"No clue and none of my business. They don't pay us to meddle, just to clean up their problems. All they told me was to find out if the pilot knew who Stone called before the crash. The client stressed that several times."

"I believe her when she says she was too busy to care."

The Boss turned his attention back to Carol. She had slumped down in the chair and almost lost consciousness while the two men talked.

"Carol, the good news is, I think you're telling the truth. I don't have any more questions for you."

"So, you'll let me go? Him too?" Carol nodded her head in Mike's direction.

"I'm sorry, but no. I can't let you go."

"Please? I promise I won't tell. I won't. Just let us go and we'll forget everything."

"That's not the way this works, Carol. It's just the way it is." The Boss nodded to one of the other men. At his signal, the black man picked up a loaded syringe and jabbed it into Carol's shoulder. She slumped forward almost immediately.

"What did he give her? Is she dead?"

"Nah, just a sedative. We're going to make this look like she committed suicide. We'll take her out to the rotating bridge and throw her in the water. The tide is going out, so she'll probably float out to sea, but if they find her body it'll look like she took some sleeping pills and then jumped. Couldn't handle the guilt of the plane crash. At least that's what the note in her hotel room will say."

"What are we going to do about him? Who is he, anyway?"

"Just some tourist who got mixed up in something he doesn't understand. We'll take him out to the West End and throw him in the water in some dive gear. It'll look like he went out by himself and didn't come back. Happens all the time."

"Does he got a shot, too? He looks like he is waking up."

"Just hit him. We don't need some medical examiner to find the sedative in his blood and get curious. Leave him in the chair and we'll come back for him when we're done with her."

#####

Mike sputtered and choked when the bucket of cold water hit his face. He quickly realized the duct tape was off of his mouth and his hands and legs were free. He started to stand up and run, but he couldn't. His legs were numb from being bound to the chair for so long. The last thing he remembered was one of the men who had Carol hitting him in the back of the head while they dragged Carol past him. *And now they're back for me*, Mike thought. *But why free me?* That didn't make sense.

"Michael, wake up. It's time to wake up."

Mike's eyes struggled to focus on the face in front of him. When they did, fear shot through his body. It was the Middle Eastern man from the hospital. Mike tried again to jump up and run, but a firm hand on his shoulder pushed him back down into the chair.

"Michael, listen to me. We are not here to hurt you. We want to help. You have to trust us right now. Where did they take the pilot? Our mission is to save her. Enough people have lost their lives over this."

"What's going on? Who are you? How did you find me?"

"My name is Ahmed. This is Jalil. As I said, we are here to help. We have been following the pilot since the plane crash and that meant following you since you interfered at the hospital. We've had you thoroughly checked out."

"What's going on?"

"Right now, we need to find the woman."

"Right now, you need to give me some answers for me to trust you."

"All right, Michael. Get some blood flowing again while I explain. But, it will have to be quick. The woman is in danger."

Mike stood up and stretched. Every inch of his body hurt and his head was pounding from being hit, but he wasn't about to fall into another trap. As he walked to the window in the warehouse, Mike could see they were on the second floor in a loft that overlooked the harbor. A large tanker ship was cruising slowly past, heading out to sea from the oil refinery.

"We are from Saudi Arabia. We work for the kingdom, but it is easier to say that we represent OPEC for now. The men who abducted you are the ones who set up the plane crash to stop Mr. Stone from meeting with the president of Venezuela. He was trying to get Venezuela to leave OPEC and sell their oil exclusively to the West. He wanted to create an OPEC of the Americas. Venezuela is 6th in production in OPEC and has the largest proved oil reserves in the world, even greater than my home nation. The country is in shambles and there is rioting in the streets so they can't produce enough oil to take advantage of it. If he had been able to convince President Arturo, it is possible he could have stabilized the country and they would have been able to increase production."

"If he had been successful, it would hurt OPEC. Why do you expect me to believe that you aren't the ones who wanted to stop him?"

"You are correct; his efforts would hurt the OPEC. But we would still be able sell our oil. If the world were to believe we caused the crash, it would turn against us. It would likely be enough to start a war. Your government, and many other nations around the world, see the price of oil as a matter of national security and any additional threat to it would awaken the sleeping giant. Right now, low oil prices make consumers happy when they fill up their SUVs and cars. But, if OPEC were seen to be manipulating things further, there would be world outrage. At the very least, political will in the United States and other countries would have turned against us and people would have rallied to stop buying OPEC oil, like after the energy crisis in the 1970s. China is one of the biggest customers and we expect their demand will only increase. There are other emerging markets as well. We could lose it all."

"Who's responsible? Who benefits from increased oil instability and turning world opinion against OPEC?"

"Mr. Stone was an unwitting pawn. His girlfriend in the US runs a large environmental group that wants to move the world away from oil entirely. If they can turn world opinion, then they feel they will have won. The last thing they want is for more cheap oil to be available and for price stability. It would not be the first time in world history that public opinion was swayed for a group to meet its goals. We know they will use any means necessary."

"And that's who he called from the plane."

"Maybe, but we are not sure. We will not know until we get the call logs. The fact that they have ordered a hit on the pilot tells us that the group doesn't want any proof of a connection between Stone and the woman."

"So, why did they sabotage the plane lift? There was an Arabic note inside the fuselage that said 'God is great!'. Why not let the plane come to the surface and that note hit the news?"

"As we have learned, that was their original intention. When they planned to bring the plane down, they wanted to imply that it was a terrorist act, so they wrote 'Allahu Akbar' inside the plane. When you rescued the pilot, that changed everything. There was a living connection to the crash and someone who might know what Stone did in his last moments. Someone who might know who he called."

"You're saying this is a set up. You've been framed. I get the politics of it, but that's a lot of effort to take against someone who 'might' know what happened."

"They needed to stop Stone, but also keep everyone confused for a few more days. The other nations of OPEC are planning a new strategy that will include Venezuela and should stabilize the situation there. But it has to happen within the framework of the regular OPEC meeting. The environmental group had to stop Stone, but they also want to keep the nations of OPEC off balance as well. They couldn't take the risk that their plotting would be exposed. One more death, that should have happened in the plane crash, was not a big leap. Now, Michael, I really must insist that we go find Ms. Anderson and free her. We have talked long enough. For all we know, she is dead by now."

"You're right, Ahmed. Carol is in danger and it's time to go, but I don't think she's dead yet."

"How do you know that?"

"I overheard the men who took her saying they were going to throw her off the bridge to make it look like a suicide. But they can't do that yet, because the bridge is closed to foot traffic right now. An oil tanker just came through. I saw that and knew she would be safe for a little while longer. I don't really trust anyone at the moment so I had to make sure you were who you say you are."

"Are you satisfied?"

"Enough for now, but it's definitely time to go. I see the bridge swinging back into place across the harbor."

#####

Carol was confused. She seemed to be walking and could hear voices around her, but she couldn't make out what they were saying. The lights were bright, overpowering everything around and making stars in her eyes. Rough hands had forced her down onto a seat and then bodies hemmed her in, blocking out the view of her surroundings. Her eyes closed and she was sure she was on a crowded subway train; the crowd, the smell of sweat and the swaying underneath her feet.

The next thing she knew, those same rough hands pulled her to her feet and she was walking. Carol didn't remember doing it, but must have dozed off on the train. She wasn't sure who these men were, but she wished they wouldn't hold her arms so tightly. It was beginning to hurt. Carol heard someone shout her name, but the voice seemed to be coming from a tunnel. It didn't seem real. She wondered if she was still asleep and dreaming. *Maybe I can wake up*, she thought. *I think I need to wake up.* But nothing changed. Until they stopped moving. Suddenly Carol wasn't on a crowded train any more. Now she was outside and looking out at the water.

How did I get here? What is going on? This is a really strange dream.

Carol heard someone shout her name again. It was closer this time. But she still couldn't tell who it was or where it was coming from. She could hear other voices, too. It was the men holding her. Fear started rising in her mind. Something was wrong. It was on the edge of her memory. She knew she was in trouble, but she couldn't remember why. Everything was hazy.

######

Mike, Ahmed and Jalil reached the base of the bridge just as Carol and her captors got to the middle. Mike shouted Carol's name and took off running. He knew without question what they had planned and he had to stop them. He remembered Carol being drugged so he didn't think she would be able to swim on her own. Ahmed and Jalil were right behind him.

#####

"What do we do?"

"We finish the job. The woman has to die. It won't look like a suicide anymore, but at least the job will be finished. Push her in the water and let's get out of here. Do everything you can to slow those guys down."

The voices didn't make sense to Carol. A woman was about to die. Push her in. What were they talking about? Who were they trying to slow down?

For a brief moment, Carol felt like she was flying. And then the water closed over her head and she began to panic.

#####

They were still 50 yards away when the men pushed Carol into the water. Mike saw two of the men draw handguns and take aim at him.

"Michael, duck down!" It was Jalil shouting. Gunfire erupted from both directions as Mike crouched. The men sent to kill Carol shot at them while the men from OPEC returned fire. They were still too far away from each other to have much chance of hitting anything, but that didn't stop them from trying. Mike wasn't carrying a gun, but he was no stranger to being shot at in war zones. He didn't like the feeling there, or here, but he was determined to get to Carol.

Four of the men who had kidnapped him and Carol started backing away now that Carol was in the water. The fifth, the one Mike had named the Boss, stayed by the railing and watched to make sure Carol was gone. Mike knew he was going to have to go through him to save her. He made up his mind and took off running again. He would let Ahmed and Jalil keep the other four occupied and out of the way and he was going to have to take out the Boss to save Carol. He was unarmed and had been knocked around pretty hard, but losing wasn't an option. His biggest concern was that the Boss would shoot Carol in the water.

The bridge wasn't a bridge in the common sense of the word. The actual walking deck was only a few feet above the water level. That made Mike's run easier because he wasn't running uphill. He could also keep an eye on the water. It was the middle of the night and the water was black as India ink, but there were lights all along the bridge that shined down into the water. Mike was relieved to see Carol's head bob above the surface. He could hear her spitting out water and then she took a deep breath. He could see her flailing her arms and trying to stay on the surface. Those were good signs, she was still fighting, but Mike was concerned it was only temporary. With everything that had happened to her, she probably couldn't keep it up for long.

Mike saw the Boss turn back toward the water and draw his own pistol. He pointed it at Carol and fired. The bullet hit the water in front of Carol and Mike saw Carol twist from the shot. She kept fighting to live, but Mike could tell she was slowing. She wasn't dead yet, but the bullet had hit her. Mike put on a burst of energy and crossed the final 10 yards between him and the Boss before the man was able to fire his weapon again. Mike dived through the air and hit the Boss in a flying tackle. They tumbled to the ground together in a tangled pile.

The Boss reacted to Mike's attack quickly and hit Mike in the side of the head with his fist. He attempted to bring his gun up to shoot Mike, but Mike kept his arms wrapped up. Still, Mike knew he wasn't going to be able to fight the man for long. He had been through a rough few hours as well. The man was strong and well-trained. Mike was fit from a life of activity traveling the world as a photojournalist, but he wasn't a trained fighter. The man twisted and kicked Mike off him, freeing himself from Mike's hold. Mike landed on something on the ground. It was hard and dug into his back. Rolling over, Mike realized it was the backpack the Red Cross had given Carol in the hospital. The bag also included something the Red Cross would never put there. Carol had dropped the gun they took from her attacker in the hotel into the bag and no one had thought to search it. They brought the bag along to set the stage for her suicide.

Before Mike could raise up and defend himself, the Boss kicked Mike in the ribs rolling him over. As he did, Mike saw Carol's head sink below the surface. She was going to die. Mike raised up on his hands and knees while his hand fumbled for the zipper on the bag. The Boss moved closer for another kick while Mike's hand found the handle of the pistol at the bottom of the bag. The man swung his leg at Mike, but Mike dodged the blow, falling onto his side. In the same motion, he flicked off the safety on the handgun and squeezed the trigger. Mike fired the gun through the bottom of the backpack and hit the Boss in the leg planted on the ground. The man crumpled to the ground.

Mike stood up and shouted at the Boss. "Don't do it! It's over." The Boss ignored Mike. He gripped his own gun and started to raise it up from the floor of the bridge. The man was not going to quit. Mike didn't have time for another struggle. He raised his own gun and prepared to fire.

Suddenly, Mike heard a gunshot, but it wasn't from his gun, or the one in the Boss' hand. The Boss slumped down. Dead. Jalil came running up. He was wounded from the shootout with the other men, but he had taken the shot on the Boss.

"Get in the water. Do it now. You must save her!" Jalil shouted.

Mike didn't hesitate. He dropped the gun to the bridge deck and leapt over the railing onto a pontoon. He took a moment to still his breathing and then stepped out into the water. Carol had gone down a few feet away from where he was.

######

The warm western Caribbean water closed over Mike's head as he dropped into the dark water in the harbor below but he didn't have time to enjoy the sensation. The darkness below him immediately robbed his senses of all stimuli except for the warmth. He couldn't see and he couldn't hear. He just hoped he would be able to touch Carol in the water. If not, it would be like finding a needle in a haystack with his eyes closed. He would have to slap his hands around in the water until he hit the mark. Worst of all, his body was already starting to demand that he breathe.

Mike piked his body and began swimming downward. He had to get to Carol quickly. As he descended through the water, Mike did his best to calm his body and focus on the task at hand. His mind brought up memories of his dive into the acrylic tank to save Ridian, the boy at the circus camp just a few days before. That dive had been successful. He found Ridian quickly and brought the boy to the surface. Rescuers at the top of the tank were able to grab him and start providing aid. It worked out exactly as it should. But doubts started flooding in on him pushing out those positive memories. Ridian had fallen into the water in an acrylic tank. That meant he could only go so far away. And the lights were on. Mike couldn't rely on Carol being anywhere. She could have drifted away from the spot where she went down. In the dark, there was no way to tell. And he didn't know how deep the water was where the bridge crossed the harbor. It probably wasn't terribly deep, but it had to be deep enough for oil tankers to pass through. That meant it wasn't shallow either.

Then I will just have to find Carol before she hits the bottom, Mike thought. Now snap out of it and do what you came here for! You didn't come all this way to lose.

Mike judged he was deep enough that he had probably caught up with Carol. He was actively swimming down and she was floating unconsciously. He started flailing around with his arms and legs, hoping to make contact with something, anything that would tell him which way to go.

The urge to breathe was nearly overwhelming. Mike swallowed to try to quiet the sensation. It worked for a moment. His run across the bridge and the fight with the Boss had robbed him of any reserves he might have had. His head began to swim and he thought for a moment he might lose consciousness. *Wouldn't that be something*, he thought, *to die while trying to save Carol. I might as well give up. I'm not going to make it and I'm not even going to make it back to the surface myself.*

Mike's hand brushed something. He wasn't sure what it was, but the rush of adrenaline that surged through his body at the feeling brought him back to reality. He still needed to breathe, badly, but at least he had some hope. He lunged forward in the direction where he made contact and found her. He slipped an arm around Carol's lifeless body, underneath her arms and pulled her close to him. He had her. Now he just had to get to the surface.

One step at a time. Kick. Pull. Stroke. Swallow. He wasn't going to give up. There was no way he was going to quit.

Kick.

Pull.

Stroke.

His free arm felt like lead. His legs wouldn't work right. Mike imagined Carol was pulling him downward. His mind started to shut down and he couldn't tell which way was up.

Mike felt an explosion in the water beside him. It shook him off balance and he nearly lost his grip on Carol's body. *The men are back! They came back to finish the job!*

Mike couldn't go anymore. He had far exceeded his limits and his brain shut down as he broke the surface.

#####

The explosion in the water wasn't the bad guys at all. Rescuers had jumped into the water to save him. One man grabbed Mike as he lost consciousness and a second took Carol from him as well. Mike had gotten them to within two feet of the surface when his body shut down. He had a shallow water blackout. Bystanders quickly dragged Mike and Carol out of the water and began resuscitating them. The next sound Mike heard were sirens coming toward them as ambulances arrived.

"What happened? What's going on?" Mike asked groggily after choking and spitting out a mouthful of seawater.

"I don't know. We heard noises that sounded like gun shots, but then someone shouted that two people had fallen off the bridge. My husband and I came running. Now, you just need to lie still and let the paramedics take care of you."

"Wait, I know you."

"By golly, you're right. I'm Myra. You photographed me and Doug out on the dive boat before the plane crash."

"It's incredible you're here. Thank you," Mike said. He tried to sit up. "Did Carol make it?"

"Yes, they got her, too. She has a nasty cut on her side and she hasn't regained consciousness yet, but she's breathing on her own."

"What about Ahmed and Jalil? And the other men? What happened to them?"

"No one was here when we got here. We just heard someone yell and we came running. We saw some men running away, but we didn't get a look at them."

"At least they're gone."

CHAPTER FOURTEEN

Mike walked along the Otrobanda quarter of Willemstad. Otrobanda literally meant "the other side" from the Punda quarter, the original walled settlement of the colonial city. He stared at the warm, inviting waters of St. Anna Bay and laughed to himself. "Warm and inviting" were not words that would have come to his mind two days before when he nearly drowned there. The sun was shining and a gentle breeze blew across the island, making it a perfect day.

The Otrobanda side gave Mike a view of the brightly colored buildings and the tourists walking along the Queen Emma Bridge to the shops and cafes along the water front. What a difference a couple days made.

Mike's fixer arrived at the hospital about the same time the medics got there with Mike and Carol. The woman quickly took charge of the situation, organizing security around their rooms and making sure there would be no more problems.

Things had been touch and go for Carol for a while, but in the hospital things she immediately began to improve and she regained consciousness the next morning. Nearly drowning twice in two days didn't make her happy, but she was happy to be alive.

Once the doctors had confirmed that Mike was fine and wouldn't have any residual problems that some rest wouldn't take care of, he quickly made a complete statement to the local police, as well as the NTSB investigators, about what had happened. Agents from the FBI were on their way to the island and he had to give them another statement the next day.

It turned out the police car used in the chase had been stolen from the maintenance garage. There was no evidence that the hit team had any connection to the police at all, although the police commissioner promised a full investigation to make sure.

They found the Boss' body floating off shore the next day. He had died from the gunshot wounds, delivered by Mike and Jalil. Jalil's shot had been the actual cause of death. Whoever tossed him in the water had stripped his body of all identification. Mike told the police that he had been an American and behaved as if he had military training so they quickly took fingerprints and DNA samples to the US military DNA registry to find out who he was.

The FBI quickly took charge of the entire investigation. They wanted to catch the international hit team that had brought down the flight, but a higher priority was the person who hired the team in the first place. Manipulating world markets was a serious criminal offense and a number of countries were interested in the outcome. Of course, conspiracy to commit murder and attempted murder were just as serious. What Ahmed told Mike wasn't enough for an arrest, but it gave the investigators a place to look and the threads of the conspiracy quickly began to unravel. Stone's girlfriend and her organization were going to be under a microscope.

Ahmed and Jalil were nowhere to be found. Mike was sure they were the ones who had yelled for help and probably even pulled Mike to the surface, but they had slipped away in the confusion once he and Carol made it to the surface. He wasn't sure about those two. Something told him that if the situation had been different and Mike had posed a threat to their employer, they would just as easily have let him die. Still, they had saved his life, along with Carol's, so that was something.

Although she was less than pleased about her star photographer and adventurer nearly getting himself killed while on vacation, Mike's editor at *First Account* Magazine was thrilled with his first person account of what had happened. A reporter had been on the way, and he had arrived on the same flight as the FBI agents. The young man was thrilled with what became an exclusive story for him that involved the oil industry, an international hit team and misguided attempts to control world markets. Half-jokingly, he told Mike he would be buying the photographer beers for the rest of both of their lives.

Considering that Mike's vacation had turned into a working trip, Mike's editor had offered to pick up his expenses and delay his trip to Brazil. Mike declined both, but he did ask a favor. He had made a promise to himself that he would fix up the Jeep he had stolen to make their get-away from the hotel. His editor quickly agreed to help out. The Jeep was returned to the owner with a new windshield and the wiring harness fixed where Mike had hotwired the vehicle. They threw in some additional upgrades and body work as well. Mike was a Jeep guy himself and wanted the poor guy to come out of this ordeal better than when it had started.

Mike stopped his walk for a few minutes to watch a group of cab drivers playing dominoes under a pavilion. They were probably supposed to be out picking up fares, but Mike knew the game of dominoes was a passion in the Caribbean and these men took the game seriously. He had seen it happen many times before, but it was still a wonder how everyday life goes on as if nothing had happened when not more than 100 yards from where he stood Mike had been in a fight for his life. That was the way of the world.

Everything was quickly coming to a close for this adventure. At least as far as he was concerned with it anyway. He was sure the investigation would go on for a while and he hoped people would go to jail for everything that had happened.

Mike had taken Carol to the airport that morning. They had parted with promises to get together again soon, although Mike knew that was unlikely. The private charter company wanted her to get back in the pilot seat quickly and his own career still had him traveling to distant lands. Of course, considering his travels it was never a bad thing to have a friend who was a pilot. He was glad everything had turned out as well as it did for her. She had been released from the hospital with no ill effects and felt good when she left. Mike was certain she would need some therapy to work through everything that had happened, but the charter company representative who came to Curacao had been nothing but supportive of her.

Mike looked at the Queen Emma bridge again. A group of tourists were walking past the exact spot where he had fought with the Boss and then jumped in the water to save Carol. Two men broke off from the group and stopped to look out across the water. Then they did something completely unexpected. The turned and looked directly at Mike. It was Ahmed and Jalil. The two men waited until they were sure Mike saw them and then they waved and tipped their hats toward him in a final salute. Mike started to run after them to learn more about what had happened after the medics arrived, but he knew he would never get to them in time. They were professionals and were not about to let themselves get caught. Especially not by a journalist.

Mike simply nodded back and smiled.

Shouts from the domino table as one man won caused Mike to look away for a moment. When he looked back to the bridge where the two men had stood, they were gone. Something told Mike he would see them again somewhere down the road.

Word of mouth is crucial for any author to succeed. If you enjoyed this book, please leave a review at Amazon even if it's only a line or two; it would make all the difference and would be very much appreciated.

Say Hello!

Eric talks about adventure and taking time to be creative, along with diving and writing, on his blog at www.booksbyeric.com. He would love it if you dropped by to say hello.

You can also follow him on Twitter, get in touch on Facebook or through Google+. Lastly, you can always send him an email: eric@booksbyeric.com

ABOUT THE AUTHOR

Life is an adventure for Eric Douglas, above and below the water and wherever in the world he ends up. Eric received a degree in Journalism from Marshall University. After working in local newspapers, honing his skills as a story teller, and following a stint as a freelance journalist in the former Soviet Union, he became a dive instructor. The ocean and diving have factored into all of his fiction works since then.

As a documentarian, Eric has worked in Russia, Honduras and most recently in his home state of West Virginia, featuring the oral histories of West Virginia war veterans in the documentary West Virginia Voices of War and the companion book Common Valor.

Visit his website at: www.booksbyeric.com.

Other books by Eric Douglas:

Mike Scott Adventures

Cayman Cowboys
Flooding Hollywood
Guardians' Keep
Wreck of the Huron
Heart of the Maya

Return to Cayman: Paradise Held Hostage
Mike Scott Thriller Boxed Set (First Five Novels)

Children's Books

Sea Turtle Rescue and Other Stories

Withrow Key Short Stories

The complete Withrow Key Collection: Tales from Withrow Key

Going Down with the Ship
Bait and Switch
Put It Back
Frog Head Key
Queen Conch

Sea Monster
Caesar's Gold
Life Under the Sea
Lyin' Fish

River Town

Non-fiction

Capturing Memories: How to Record Oral Histories
Keep on, Keepin'on: A Breast Cancer Survivor Story
Common Valor: Companion to the multimedia documentary West Virginia Voices of War
Russia: The New Age
Scuba Diving Safety

Mike Scott will be back in the novel *Summer of the Shark*!

Made in the USA
Middletown, DE
26 September 2016